P9-EDF-170

WASHINGTON AND BALTIMORE

WASHINGTON

AND

BALTIMORE

Stories by

JULIAN MAZOR

New York: ALFRED · A · KNOPF

[1968]

THIS IS A BORZOI BOOK
PUBLISHED BY ALFRED A. KNOPF, INC.

 Distributed by Random House, Inc. Published simultaneously in Toronto, Canada, by Random House of Canada Limited. Manufactured in the United States of America.

Library of Congress Catalog Card Number: 68-14883

"Washington," "Baltimore," "Rock Creek," and "The Boy Who Used Foul Language" were first published in *The New Yorker*; "Mary Jane" was originally published in *Shenandoah*.

FIRST EDITION

TO

William Shawn

and to Arra Ann

and to my mother and father

CONTENTS

Washington

WHEN I RAN through Pennsylvania Station on a cloudy November afternoon, I was wearing a clean blue shirt with a soft unbuttoned collar, a brown knit tie, a brown herringbone suit, well-polished brown Spanish shoes, and an English overcoat—a gray herringbone—that I had worn for three years. I had some old letters stuffed into the inside pocket of my jacket, and after I had taken out my wallet to buy my train ticket I had trouble putting it back. I was afraid I would miss my train, so I slipped the wallet into the inside pocket of my overcoat, thinking I would sort things out when I was aboard. I had a hundred and forty-seven dollars in the wallet, a sum left over from my last pay check, and I was on my way to Washington, D.C., to see my family—my mother and father and an older sister who had recently got married. I had just left my job as a salesman-demonstrator-instructor in the tennis department of a famous New York department store, where I, John Lionel, was known as "Wright & Ditson." One day, for some reason, while demonstrating the proper service technique to a twelve-year-old boy and his mother, I tossed a tennis ball up in the air and hit a powerful cannonball service; the ball whizzed by the floor manager's —Mr. Palmerston's—ear, and smashed a glass case. Palmerston said it was nice knowing me and told me to pick up my check. So long, Wright & Ditson. It was my third job since coming back from Europe, where I had served a tour in the Army, and although in a way I was a little concerned because I didn't seem to be going anywhere and didn't know where I wanted to go, I thought, Well, I'm only twenty-three and I've got time.

Somewhere near North Philadelphia, I ate a tuna-fish sandwich that I bought from a vender on the train, and about twenty minutes south of the Thirtieth Street Station I began to feel warm and a little strange. I thought I'd get some air, so I left my seat and went out to the platform between the cars. I leaned against the steel wall and smoked and looked out at the countryside. The cool air made me feel a lot better. I stayed out between the cars until the train was about a half hour past Wilmington, and then I returned to my seat in the coach.

I thought I'd get a book out of my suitcase and read for a while. When I looked up at the baggage rack, I saw that my overcoat was gone. I had forgotten to take the wallet out of it. I had placed the coat neatly folded over my suitcase, and there was no doubt that it was gone. I walked up and down the coach, looking at all the overcoats in the baggage racks, and then I returned to my seat and tried to be calm and think things out. Then I went up and down the car again. When I returned to my seat for the second time, feeling demoralized and enraged, a man sitting across the aisle asked me what was the matter, and I told him that my overcoat was gone. The man folded his newspaper and looked out the window for a while, and then he asked me to describe the coat. I told him that it was a gray herringbone, and that it had been on the rack above my seat. He took a deep breath and let it out slowly, and then, seeming embarrassed, he told me that he had seen a man pull my coat from the rack as the train got into Wilmington, and that he had, even then, found it a little strange, because this man was already wearing a camel's-hair coat.

I slumped down in my seat, feeling sick. I always do when somebody steals from me. For a while, I sat there thinking about my overcoat and how it had been part of the friendly continuity of my life. Then I got to my feet and went through my pockets and came up with fifty cents. I had lost my money, my Social Security card, and even my passport. I began to feel cold and hot alternately, and around Aberdeen I began to feel cramps and nausea. I figured it was the tuna-fish sandwich. Just outside of Baltimore, I became desperately sick and went to the men's room and threw up. I was sick again between Baltimore and Washington, and when the train finally pulled into Union Station and I stepped out into the cold, rainy afternoon, I felt like hell.

I didn't have enough money for a cab, and it was no use calling home. My family was out of town, visiting my sister's husband's family in Maryland. They would be coming back to Washington in the morning. So I got on a bus, and about twenty minutes later got off, in the rain, and transferred to another bus. While I was on the bus, the nausea and cramps came back and I decided I'd have to get off. I began to look for a bar or restaurant or hotel along the way, and when I saw a gasoline station in a very old, shabby neighborhood—a Negro neighborhood—I pulled the cord and picked up my suitcase and got off.

In the men's room of the gasoline station, I bathed my face in cold water, and went outside again. I was feeling much better, but weak. The rain was cold, and the wind had grown stronger, and I was shivering. I was about to cross the street and wait by a little yellow bus-stop sign, when I saw that I was in front of a small grocery store with a green awning slanting down over a dimly lighted display window. I decided to stand under the awning and watch for the bus from there.

INSIDE THE grocery store, three Negroes were leaning against a long, white refrigerated case, or counter, talking and laughing. Another Negro, in a white apron, was behind the counter, leaning on it and reading a newspaper and eating a sandwich. I thought of going into the store and getting warm, but I had no excuse for going in, really—no money to buy anything with. So I stayed under the awning, which was flapping wildly in the wind. My teeth were chattering, and I felt a sore throat coming on, when I saw a Negro man and woman walking down the street in the rain, arguing. They'd walk without speaking, then stop and argue, then walk some more. Actually, it was more of a dramatic exercise than an argument. The woman would make wordless faces at the man, which unsettled him. He would get ready to say something, and then she would laugh at him. Then he would look surprised and cautious, as though he was searching for a little balance and leverage, and she would scream at him. Then she would tell him to shut up, and he would look surprised, and finally he would begin to scream at her, and then she would begin to laugh at him, which made him more unsteady. The man was squat and round, with a black moonface crowned by a porkpie hat. He was wearing a frayed and very wet fatigue jacket. His companion was mocha brown, and tall and wide. She was large-boned and hefty, but not fat, and although she was obviously strong, she was unmistakably feminine. She wore a man's raincoat and a pair of bedroom slippers without backs. She didn't wear stockings, and she didn't wear a hat. She had a wide nose and a wide mouth, and large, beautiful eyes. She walked ahead of the man into the grocery store, slamming the door after her, and he followed her in, looking worried and confused.

I leaned my back against the window and watched the rain water pour off the awning and splash over my shoes. I was standing in a puddle about an inch deep, but it hardly mattered any more. I was beginning to feel sick again. There was no sign of the bus. To take my mind off myself, I turned and faced the window, and I saw the woman dancing around the store with her arms outstretched and her eyes half closed. The men standing near the refrigerated case kept up a rhythmic clapping. She went on dancing around, having a marvelous time, while the man in the porkpie hat looked sullenly at the floor.

After a while, I turned around and faced the street again. I felt like a shipwreck hanging on a reef, or a piece of driftwood. I think I had a touch of delirium. I was thinking about what to do next, when the woman and the man in the porkpie hat came out of the grocery store.

"You deny that? You deny that?" he yelled at her. He was standing next to me under the awning.

"Go on, man. Go on. Go on," she said, walking away from him and moving indifferently into the rain.

"Now, you deny that?" he said. "Now where you going? You come on back here."

"You don't own me, baby," she said, walking on.

He gave a few preliminary grunts of frustration, and then he began to scream at her to come back, but she paid no attention to him. "You hear me? I'm talking to you! You come on back here," he said.

Halfway down the block, she stopped and turned around, put her hands on her hips, yelled something obscene at him, and then stretched out her arms and began to laugh.

"Honey, you getting wet. Now, you come on back here," he called imploringly.

She yelled something at him again.

"Now, honey, why you talk that way to me?" he yelled.

"Man, leave me alone. You make me sick," she said, moving on.

"Come on, honey, you know I don't feel good," he cried at her in a sad whine.

THE WOMAN crossed the street quickly, and the man watched her, moving his mouth without saying anything. He seemed too tired to go after her. For a while, he stood with his arms folded and shook his head. He didn't seem to know that I was there, even though only about a foot separated us. I was slightly behind him, still leaning against the window, when he turned around and looked surprised; then he closed his mouth and narrowed his eyes and looked angry.

"How are you?" I said.

"What you say?" he asked, putting a hand over his eyes.

"I said, 'How are you?' "

He held his hand over his eyes, considering the question. "That ain't what you said," he told me finally, still covering his eyes.

"O.K., that's not what I said."

I looked down at my feet, at the puddle I was standing in, trying to ignore him. I noticed that he was wearing a ripped pair of black, misshapen shoes and no socks, and that his pants legs were rolled up a little above his ankles. Suddenly he jumped into the puddle I was standing in and splashed me. I couldn't believe it.

"Now, what did you say?" he asked, folding his arms.

I didn't answer.

"You trying to make a fool out of me?" he asked.

"I'm not trying to make a fool out of you," I said. I looked down the street, feeling sick and desperate, but the street was empty and it was raining harder than ever.

"You mean you ain't trying but I am a fool anyhow. Right?" he said.

"I didn't say that."

"But that what you mean," he said. "You a wise guy. Right?"

"I'm just waiting for a bus. If I insulted you, it was unintentional," I said.

"Don't give me unintentional. I unintentional *you*."

He kicked the puddle, splashing my pants with water, and said he was going to knock me down. Then he stepped back, dropping his hands to the level of his belt, and measured me. I picked up my suitcase and moved it a few feet, setting it on a narrow ledge just below the window.

"Man, I'm gonna wipe you out," he said, opening and closing his hands several times.

I took a deep breath and let it out slowly. He looked very strong, and I am of medium height and rather frail. "Well," I said, "you're going to have the worst fight of your life."

"You gonna give it to me?" he asked, smiling.

I told him that I was going to beat the hell out of him, and then I brought my hands up.

"Man, will you look at that!" he said. "This is gonna be some fun."

He touched the brim of his hat, dropped his hands into position again, and, five feet away from me, began to bob and weave. "You come on in," he said. "I'm a counterpuncher."

I didn't move, but watched him closely, keeping my hands high. I told him I was a counterpuncher, too. He began to circle me, and I turned with him. He kept on going through this little shadowboxing routine, paying only nominal attention to me. He looked very good, very agile.

After a few minutes of circling and jabbing and hooking at the air, he stopped and looked at me. "You looks terrible," he said. We had maneuvered ourselves out into the rain, and the water was streaming over our faces. "You off balance," he said.

I told him not to worry about it, that I had fast hands and a good punch.

"The only thing you doing right is standing up," he said, shaking his head. He held up his hands in a truce gesture and walked over to me. He said he wanted to give me some basic instruction. He adjusted my hands slightly and pushed my head down so that it was protected by my left shoulder, and then he kicked my feet to a different position, saying I was standing flat-footed. "Now you looking good," he said.

"Well, it feels unnatural," I said, resuming my old position.

Then, to prove that my style was poor, he asked me to try to hit him. He said he wouldn't try to hit me but would just give me a little demonstration that would do more for me than all the talk in the world.

"I don't want to hit you," I said.

"Don't worry, you ain't going to," he said.

"Look, I'll take your word for it," I said.

"Come on, now," he said. "You got to see what I mean to really believe it."

So he began to bob and weave with his hands low, presenting his head as a slowly moving target. I watched his head bob for about thirty seconds, and tried to measure him. He kept talking the whole time. "You can't get set, see. Now you see it, now you don't. You all tied up."

I pulled my right hand back a few inches, and he broke into a wide grin, and then, while he was grinning, I feinted with my right hand and came hard with a left hook, catching him squarely on the side of the jaw. He whirled around and pitched forward on the pavement, landing hard on his chest and then rolling over on his side. He wasn't hurt. He grabbed his hat and jumped quickly to his feet, looking annoyed and embarrassed. "I'll be goddam," he said, one hand on top of his hat.

"I'm very sorry," I said. "Are you all right?"

"Some rain got in my eye," he said. "I ain't seen your left."

He said he wanted to give me a few more demonstrations, but I told him I'd had enough. I suddenly felt sick again, with the hot-and-cold business returning—the nausea and cramps and the rest. My legs became weak. Feeling I was going to faint, I walked over to the window and leaned against it. I decided to forget about the bus, for the time being, and go back to the men's room in the gasoline station. I took up my suitcase and started to walk away, when the man trotted over and grabbed me by the arm. "Where you going?" he asked.

"I'm not feeling well," I said, jerking my arm away. "Leave me alone."

"Man, what's wrong with you?" he asked, smiling. "You knock me down and *you* is mad."

Then he began to throw a flurry of punches at the air in front of me, bobbing and weaving, going into a series of strange forward and lateral hops and skips, dancing, and finally winding it up by running in place. I think he felt he was cheering me up, for he kept up the running for about two minutes, making faces, and then he stopped and said, "*Now* how you feeling?"

I told him to get out of my way, but he continued to block me, and I was too weak to try to run around him.

He jumped up in the air and closed his eyes and flapped his arms. "*Now* how you feeling?" he asked, after a few jumps.

I told him I was feeling worse than ever, and that if he really wanted to help me he would go away and leave me alone.

He said that I was just a little down and out, and there was nothing to worry about if I listened to him. He told me about his Opposite Theory. "If you feel like lying down, then stand up," he said. "If you feel like crying, then laugh."

I tried to get by him, but he grabbed me by the shoulder of my coat. "Maybe if you lie down you never get up. You thought of that?"

I broke away and started to run, but he caught up with me easily and clapped a huge hand on my shoulder and pressed down. I whirled around, dropped my suitcase, and threw a wild right hand at him, but he ducked under it neatly and countered, though intentionally missing, with a classic one-two. "Sickness all in the mind," he said.

I told him my sickness was in the stomach and that he should get the hell away from me, but he shook his head, half closing his eyes. "I ain't gonna let you give in to it," he said. "I gonna help you fight it."

He said he knew all about the body, because he was an ex-fighter, and most ex-fighters knew more about the human body than any doctor, and that every man has a secret place in him which fights sickness and pain, and the trick was to have faith in that secret place. He said you had to turn on that little secret power by doing just the opposite of what your body asked you to do.

While he was talking, I developed a headache, and I was about to ask him what this headache was telling me to do, so I could do the opposite, when I began to see objects in pairs and threes, and I knew I was going to fall. The nausea was so bad that I couldn't keep my mouth closed, and the ground seemed to tilt. I dropped down on one knee, pushing at the ground with both hands. "Get up," I heard him say, his voice far off. "Is you gonna lay down? Is you gonna quit?"

As I pushed at the ground, fighting it and the nausea, a bus went by, and the next thing I knew the man was grabbing me under the arms and pulling me to my feet. "We gonna make it," he said.

I tried to push him away. I succeeded in breaking free of one hand, but he had me by the collar with the other. "You doing fine," he said. "You got to keep moving around. It good for the circulation." The word "circulation" seemed to give him an idea, for he began to slap my face with his free hand.

I called him a stupid son of a bitch, hit him hard on the mouth, lurched and spun away from him, hearing my coat and shirt rip, and fell onto the pavement, where I crawled to the gutter and threw up. He stood near me. He kept saying, "You doing fine. You doing fine. You gonna be a new man now. We gonna clear you out."

As he was talking, the street lamps came on. I looked over at him and watched the rain bounce off his shoes. One of his pants legs had come unrolled in the scuffle, and the cuff was ripped.

"How you doing?" he asked, smiling, getting down on one knee and putting his hand on my forehead. His lip was bleeding. I knocked his hand away, and looked down at the fast-moving water in the gutter.

"Man, I is wounded," he said. He leaned over the gutter and brought some water up for his bloodied lip.

"Look, I'm gonna tell you a joke," he went on. I got up and started to walk back to the awning, and he followed me, taking my suitcase from my hand and carrying it for me. "This man, he in a restaurant, and he say, 'Waiter, there is a fly in the soup,' and this waiter, he say, 'Don't worry, he can swim.' "

He began to laugh. We stood under the awning, and he continued to laugh at his joke while I looked down the street for the bus. He calmed down and then began to regard me seriously, putting a hand over his mouth.

"Say, you know who I am?" he asked.

I shook my head.

"I guess you heard of Ringo Brown," he said, "who fight in Griffith Stadium in 1939, '40, '41, and '46."

"If you're Ringo Brown, I never heard of you," I said.

"Aw, come on, man," he said, smiling. "I fight twenty-three preliminaries and one main event. I lose the main event. You remember Red Hickey, from Delaware?"

"No."

"I lose to him in a split decision. He was a good boy, but he never did nothing. I was a middleweight."

"You lost only one fight?" I said.

"Now, I ain't said that, but I never knocked out."

I pulled out a pack of cigarettes and a lighter. The pack was wet, but I managed to find two dry cigarettes, and I gave Ringo one. We smoked for a while without saying anything, and then Ringo said, "Say, kid, what's your name?"

"John," I said. "John Lionel."

I saw a bus coming, and I picked up my suitcase and began to move away.

"Where you going?" Ringo asked.

"So long, Ringo," I said.

As I started to cross the street, he came and grabbed me by the arm. "John, I carry your bag," he said. "You tired."

"I'm all right. It's not heavy," I said.

"No, I carry it."

Ringo began to fight me for the suitcase, right there in the middle of the street. He pushed me with one hand and grabbed the suitcase away with the other. I ran over to the bus stop and called back to Ringo to bring the suitcase. The bus had stopped and was letting off passengers. Ringo just smiled at me from the other side of the street. I asked the driver to wait a second, but he took one look at me and closed the door and drove off. I walked over to Ringo and took the suitcase from him. "You're crazy," I said.

"They be another bus, John," he said, smiling. "One as good as another."

I walked back to the bus stop and decided to wait there, even though the rain was coming down harder than ever. Ringo followed me. "I try to do you a good turn and you don't let me. Don't you know that hurt?" he said.

"Get away from me!"

"Won't even let me carry his suitcase across the street," Ringo said, shaking his head.

He remained standing by me, his arms folded across his chest. I was beginning to feel faint again—not sick, only weak and tired and a little dizzy—and I put my hand over my face.

"Let's go to Billy's and have a sandwich," he said, slapping me on the shoulder. He pointed to the grocery store across the street.

"No, thanks," I said.

He said that a sandwich would build up my strength, and that he was hungry.

"I've only got a quarter," I said, "and that's for the bus."

"You can clean up at Billy's. He got a bathroom," Ringo said. "You can watch for the bus inside the store and keep warm. You can dry off some."

I didn't say anything.

"Come on, John," he said. And then he grabbed my suitcase again and ran off across the street with it and into Billy's. I was so damned mad I slammed my hand against the bus-stop post, and then I followed Ringo across the street and into the grocery store.

"HERE I AM, Billy," Ringo was saying when I went in.

"Yeah, I see you," a slight, light-brown Negro said. He was the one in the white apron. The three Negroes leaning against the refrigerated case were smiling. Billy looked at Ringo, then at me, then back at Ringo.

"Now what you getting mad at? You mad at me, Billy?" Ringo said.

"What you doing with that suitcase?" Billy asked. "You going to catch a train?"

"Ain't this Union Station?" Ringo said, smiling at everyone.

"You ain't funny, Ringo. You just ain't funny," Billy said. "Give this man his suitcase."

"You got to be serious about everything. Nobody can

take a joke," Ringo said, handing me the suitcase without looking at me.

"We seen the whole thing," Billy said. "We seen this man drop you, Ringo." Billy looked at me. "He deserved it," he said.

"You got that same tricky style, Ringo," one of the other Negroes said.

"He sure know how to fall," Billy said. "He an expert at that."

"Aw, man," Ringo said. "We wasn't in no fight. I teaching him some things."

"Yeah, you a real teacher, all right," Billy said. "You teach any man alive how to fall. But fighting something else."

Billy smiled at the other men, and then he looked at me. "You been sick, right?" he said.

I said yes, that I had an upset stomach. Billy said there was a bathroom in the back of the store, and that I could use it if I wanted to. I thanked him and said that I would like to clean up.

"I give you something for your stomach when you come back," Billy said. He took my suitcase and put it behind the counter, and then he led me back to the bathroom and switched on the light for me.

When I got back from the bathroom, Ringo was shadowboxing in the middle of the room.

"Go. Go. Go. Hey!" one of the men said.

I walked over to Billy and stood beside him, watching the performance. Ringo was putting together some combinations to the head and body. "He won't go down. This sucker's tough," he said.

"They *all* tough, Ringo, for you," Billy said, and then he turned to me. "I lost more damn money on him," he said.

I asked Billy if Ringo had fought in Griffith Stadium.

"Yeah, I guess so," he said. "That was a long time ago. He look pretty good when there ain't nobody in his way. Say, how you feeling?" Billy looked seriously at me. I told him I was feeling a little tired.

"Well, I got something for you," he said, walking over to a shelf and taking down a large bottle of Coca-Cola syrup. He poured a little into a paper cup and handed it to me. "Drink that down and you be all right," he said.

I drank the syrup slowly and watched Ringo jump rope without a rope. His footwork was very good.

"See how his eyes is half closed," Billy said. "He really happy and stupid."

The three Negroes who had been leaning against the case stood up, nodded and smiled at Billy, and went out into the rain. Ringo continued to jump rope, but when he noticed that they had gone he seemed to lose interest. Looking distracted, as though he were trying to figure out what he could do next, he came over to Billy and me and broke out into a wide smile. "Hey, Billy, how about making me and John a sandwich," he said, tilting his head a little in a mock coyness that I hadn't seen before.

Billy turned to me, and I told him I didn't want a sandwich. Billy looked at Ringo and slowly shook his head. "Of course, you got the money. Right?" he said.

"John here, he carry the money," Ringo said.

I told Billy that all I had was a quarter.

"Even if you have the money, I ain't gonna let you buy him no sandwich," Billy said.

Ringo looked down at the floor and tapped his right foot nervously and scratched his leg. Then he put both hands over his eyes. Nothing happened. When Ringo finally took his hands away from his eyes, he said, "Billy, but I hungry."

"Hell, you always hungry, Ringo," Billy said. "But that don't mean you starving. It obvious you ain't no middleweight no more."

"That ain't nice," Ringo said, looking pained. "Why the world full of bad feeling?" He put his hands over his hat, crossing his fingers, and closed his eyes and began to twist and contort his mouth. He began to shake his whole body, without moving his feet or changing his position, and then, with his eyes still closed, he smiled. I looked over at Billy to see how he was taking it. He was leaning on the counter, reading the Washington *Post*. I went behind the counter and picked up my suitcase. Billy looked up from his paper. "Well," he said, "you *looking* better. How you *feeling?*"

"Much better," I said. "Thanks a lot, Billy." We shook hands.

"Look at that fool!" Billy said.

Ringo was still vibrating and smiling, but his eyes were open now. "What you doing with that suitcase?" he asked.

I didn't say anything, but moved toward the door to watch for another bus.

Ringo came up to me and put an arm around my shoulder. "So you going home," he said.

"That's right," I said.

"What you in a big hurry for?" he asked.

"So long, Ringo."

"I don't see no bus coming," he said.

I made sure I had a firm hold on my suitcase; then I tried to walk away, but he had a strong grip on my shoulder. "There ain't no bus coming," he said, smiling.

"Get lost, Ringo," I said.

"Go on, Ringo. Go on, now," Billy said. He came out from behind the counter.

"Look, there your bus, John," Ringo said.

I turned and looked out the window, but the street was clear. While I was looking down the street, Ringo slipped his forearm under my chin and pressed it against my throat. With his free hand he pressed the back of my head forward. "Now what you gonna do?"

I couldn't talk, because he was pressing too hard on my throat. I swung my suitcase, trying to hit him with it, but could only manage a light, slapping blow to the back of his legs.

Ringo began to laugh. "You can't do nothing, see? You can't do nothing."

Then he suddenly yelled and let me go.

I turned around, rubbing my throat, and saw Billy just back of Ringo, holding a large soda bottle. Ringo was grabbing at his ankle and hopping on one foot.

"Goddam, Billy," he said. "You nearly break my leg."

"Next time I break your head."

Ringo hopped over to the refrigerated case and sat on the front edge of it, holding his ankle. He looked from me to Billy, then back to me again. His eyes were half closed; his mouth was turned down exaggeratedly, like a clown's. "I just tired to death," Ringo said. "Man, you coulda hurt me, Billy."

"Yeah, sure," Billy said. "Now, why don't you shut up."

"I mess around," Ringo said. "But I don't hurt nobody."

"That's what you say," Billy said, putting the soda bottle back on the shelf.

I stood by the door, and finally I saw a bus turn the corner three blocks down. I pulled the quarter out of my pocket, grabbed my suitcase, and turned around for a final goodbye. "So long, Billy. Thanks," I said.

Billy waved and smiled at me. "So long, now."

As I backed through the door, I waved, knocking my hand against the doorframe. I dropped the quarter and it rolled under the refrigerated case, and I missed the bus again.

"Now, ain't that a damn shame!" Ringo said. He was all lit up, and had recovered his vitality.

Billy came over with a wooden yardstick to see if he could get the quarter out; it had become lodged between the case and the wall. He worked the yardstick in the crack until he had moved the quarter out onto the open floor. He picked it up, dusted it off on his apron, and handed it to me. "You having a bad day," he said. "Next time you keep it in your pocket." He slapped me on the back and told me I was going to make it.

Ringo looked at me with a wide and happy grin. "Well, Charlie, you having some rough luck," he said.

"My name's not Charlie," I said.

"Ain't you Charlie White Man?" Ringo said, smiling.

"Go on, Ringo. Go on," Billy said, looking at me apologetically.

"I got to admit that you is some fool, John," Ringo said, coming over to me. "You all set to go and then you drop the quarter." He laughed, closing his eyes, and put his hand on my shoulder.

I asked him if he wanted to rip the sleeve off this time.

"It look like you got a flower growing out of your shoulder," Ringo said, putting a finger on the ripped white lining that was puffing out. "Man, you look like hell. You know that?"

I took out my pack of cigarettes and lit one. Ringo watched me. I gave him the pack and told him to keep it and go away.

"You scares me," he said, taking my cigarette to light his. "I just can't figure you out."

Suddenly I got a terrible headache, and the room began to spin. Down the street another bus had appeared, but I decided it was no use even trying this time. I turned and looked at Billy, and he knew immediately that I was in some kind of trouble. "Don't you worry, now," he said. He pointed to the door that led to the bathroom. "See you soon," he said.

I walked unsteadily toward the door. There must have been a disturbance in my middle ear, because the ceiling seemed to rush at me and then rush away. I fell down, and began to crawl on all fours toward the door.

"He think he a horse," I heard Ringo say.

Billy helped me to my feet, steadied me, and walked me a few steps toward the bathroom. I told him I was all right and could make it the rest of the way. In the bathroom, I wasn't sick, but I was so dizzy that I couldn't stand up. I sat down on the floor and leaned against the wall for a few minutes, waiting for the dizziness to stop. Then I lay down and went to sleep.

Some time later, I felt someone nudging me lightly on the shoulder, and I woke up and saw Billy in his white apron, kneeling on one knee.

"You been in here about twenty minutes," he said. "I got to worry about you."

I stood up and walked over to the sink, feeling all right. The vertigo was gone. Billy switched on the light and stayed in the room while I washed up. "John, I think your luck is turning," he said.

WHEN BILLY and I went back into the big room, Ringo was talking to the woman I had seen him with earlier, outside the store. There was also another man—a large, dark-brown, sleepy-eyed Negro whom the woman called Tracy. "All right, Tracy, go on, knock him down," she said, pointing at Ringo.

Billy set a chair for me in the corner of the room farthest from Ringo and his friends. He saw that I was shivering, and he got his topcoat and told me to put it on. He also gave me another cup of Coca-Cola syrup, and said he was boiling some water for tea, and that I should just relax and take it easy.

"Knock him on his butt, Tracy," the woman said, looking fierce.

"Aw, honey, now," Tracy said, and then he smiled shyly at Ringo and folded his arms.

Ringo kicked some imaginary object, and turned on the woman. "Ruby, why you always want to make trouble?" he said. "Now, Tracy's my friend."

"I want to see you fight," Ruby said. "You supposed to be a fighter. Well, I want to see you fight."

Billy came over with a glass jar of tea and half a lemon. He put the tea and lemon on top of a milk crate near my chair. Then he went behind the counter and came back with a sack of granulated sugar and a spoon. "This gonna give you some strength," he said, putting the sugar and spoon on the crate.

I thanked him, and, feeling comfortable and warm, sat back and watched the action. While Billy was bringing me the tea, Ruby had hit Ringo on the side of the head with her pocketbook, and now Ringo, looking pained, ignored her, folded his arms, and stared at the ceiling.

"Come on, Tracy, knock him down," Ruby bellowed, but Tracy, who was about six feet four and two hundred and fifty pounds, just looked down at the floor and smiled. "Now, Tracy, here, done spar with Joe Louis. Now, Tracy was a fighter!" she went on. "A heavyweight!" She looked at Ringo with scorn.

There was a long pause, during which Ringo took a deep breath and closed his eyes. "It don't matter what class a man fight in," Ringo said finally. "It only matter if he any good or not." He opened his eyes and looked at Ruby. "Now, I was a good middleweight."

"Uh-uh. You only fair, baby. At the most, you only fair," she said.

Ringo suddenly began to jump rope and put together some combinations, moving around the room with a wide smile and his eyes half closed. As he passed me the first time around, he winked and said, "How you doing, John?"

Billy was talking in a hoarse whisper to Tracy and Ruby. I couldn't hear what he said to them, but they were smiling. Ruby clapped her hands and threw her head back and shrieked, "Aw, come on, man, you killing me!"

Tracy covered his mouth with one of his enormous hands, trying to stifle the laughter, but some of it got through. He seemed a little embarrassed and shook his head. During Billy's whispering, Ruby looked at me from time to time and smiled and waved. Tracy looked at me once, too, and nodded shyly. Then Billy brought them over, and when I stood up, Ruby told me to sit down and save my strength.

"John, this here is Ruby Longstreet and Tracy James," Billy said.

We shook hands.

"Well, John, we sure glad to know you," Ruby said, shaking hands again.

I told her the pleasure was all mine.

"I seen you outside earlier, John," she said.

"I was waiting for a bus."

"I hear that fool Ringo done give you a fight lesson," she said. She looked at Ringo, who closed his eyes. "Come on, Ringo, open your eyes!" she said.

But he shut them tighter, and closed his mouth tight, too.

Billy laughed. "John knock him flat," he said.

"What you hit him with?" Tracy asked me.

"A left," I said.

"He still blind to a left hand," Tracy said.

I said that some rain had got in his eye.

"Some rain always getting in his eye," Ruby said. "If it ain't for the rain, he been champion."

Billy laughed, and Tracy covered his face with his hands and shook. Ringo turned his back on us and began to take very deep, noisy breaths. "Aw, shut up, Ringo, you fat fool!" Ruby said.

I was trying to drink the tea, but I began to laugh so hard that I had to put the jar down, and then the laughter increased all around, and Ringo's breathing became noisier and his shoulders began to shake. I thought he was laughing, but he turned around and he was crying; tears were streaming down his face. "You all finish?" he asked.

"Will you look at that?" Ruby said.

I felt terribly sorry for him. "Come on, Ringo," I said. "What's the matter with you?"

"He just acting," Billy said.

Ringo pulled out a handkerchief and blew his nose and wiped his eyes, and then pulled up a crate and sat down next to me. "John, I feel lousy," he said. "How are you feeling?"

I told him I was feeling all right.

He patted me on the shoulder. "Well, I glad *you* feeling better," he said. He offered me a cigarette from the pack I had given him, and struck a match and gave me a light. "John, you my friend," he said. "They is some people don't know what friendship is." He looked around at everyone.

"Man, if you a friend," Billy said, "then there ain't no point having no enemy."

Ruby began to laugh, and she came over to Ringo

and kissed him on top of the head. "Baby, why you so stupid?" she said, smiling widely at him. "Maybe you is the dumbest man in the whole world."

This revived Ringo, and he grabbed Ruby's arm and asked her to sit down next to him and be nice. Billy brought three more milk crates over, and Tracy and Ruby sat on two of them, and then Billy brought a pack of six cans of beer and an opener. "Ringo, because you such a good friend, we gonna have a little party," Billy said.

He went to the front door and locked it. He said there wasn't any point staying open in all this rain anyhow. I drank my tea while the others drank beer, and then, feeling much better, I drank some beer, too. Ruby, holding her can of beer, announced she was going to sing a song. "I ain't Mahalia Jackson, but I can sing," she said.

She could, too. She sang a song, mostly humming it, while Ringo accompanied her with a little dance. He closed his eyes and put his hand in the pockets of his jacket and moved his feet very slowly back and forth.

"Where you coming from, John?" Ruby asked, when she had finished singing.

"New York," I said. "I came down on the train to see my family."

"Man, you have been travelling some," Tracy said, "and you still ain't home."

"When you with friends, you home. Ain't that right, John?" Ringo said.

Ruby said she liked to take train trips. "There ain't nowhere I want to go, but I *do* like the ride," she said.

She asked me if I had a good ride down, and I told them the story of my ride, how my overcoat and wallet had been stolen on the train, and how, after that, I had got sick.

"People get you sick every time," Ruby said thoughtfully.

"Sure," Billy said. "And then Ringo get you sick in Washington."

"I ain't get John sick," Ringo said. "I been helping John."

"You been *helping* John?" Ruby said. "Who else you *help* lately?"

"John ain't the only white man I ever help," Ringo said, smiling.

"Honey," Ruby said, leaning forward. "What other white man you nearly kill?"

"Few years ago I was working for this man name of Reddy," Ring said, biting the corner of his lip. "In this junk yard out northeast."

"Yeah," Bill said. "I remember you and that *junk*."

"Well, one day," Ringo said, "Mr. Reddy is standing on the street watching these colored boys working on a trash truck. They up there singing and laughing, and Mr. Reddy, he say, 'Boys, you happy. You sure is happy. You have all the fun,' and one of them colored boys, he say, 'That's right, boss. We having some fun,' and they up there tossing them trash cans around and laughing, and Mr. Reddy, he watch them and smile, and then he walk over to me and he say, 'Ringo, you colored boys sure is happy,' and I say, 'Mr. Reddy, I ain't happy. Them niggers up on that truck may be happy, but I ain't,' and he get real angry, and he say, 'Don't give me no lip, Ringo,' and I laugh. 'Well, I sure ain't happy,' I say, 'with the wages you paying.' He fire me."

Billy guffawed and Tracy put his hands over his face and began to shake.

"How you *help* him, baby?" Ruby said, looking around at everybody.

Ringo spread his arms and turned his palms upward, and then he broke into a wide smile. "Well, I straighten him *out!*" he said.

Ruby laughed and slapped her thigh. Tracy, still shaking, kept his hands over his face, while Billy just looked at the floor and smiled.

RINGO STARTED jumping rope with his eyes closed. Tracy leaned forward and touched Ruby's knee. "Ruby, you ain't gonna give that old moral?" he said, looking disgusted.

"I got to, baby," Ruby said. "O.K., Billy, you ask me."

Billy looked serious and folded his arms across his apron. "What's the moral of that story?"

"The moral of that story—" Ruby began, looking very serious.

"Aw, Ruby," Tracy said, shaking his head and looking at his feet. Ringo, with his arms straight out and his eyes closed, was standing completely still.

"The moral of that story," Ruby went on, holding up a hand for quiet, "is that, Ringo, honey, you sure is one dumb nigger."

They all began to laugh, moaning and groaning with laughter, leaning on one another, and, except for Ruby,

Ringo laughed loudest and hardest. The laughter continued for about five minutes, gradually diminishing, then rising again. Ruby had her arms around Tracy's head, and Ringo sat on the floor. Billy had walked over to the counter and, leaning on it, his hands palms down on the top, laughed in gasps. I was laughing myself.

"Now, what you laughing at?" Ringo said to me from the floor. "That ain't nice."

Ruby looked over at me and said, "Honey, don't pay us no mind."

After a while, the laughter fell into silence. There were just the sounds of the wind, and Billy's shoes on the floor, as he walked around taking cans out of cartons and putting them on shelves. Only Ruby was still smiling. Tracy and Ringo seemed sad. They were looking down at their hands. Ringo, who had a very gentle expression, was biting his lip. Billy moved around looking preoccupied and tired. Ruby looked at me and winked, and I smiled at her. She was one of the most beautiful women I have ever seen. She nodded in the direction of Tracy and Ringo, and said to me, "They looking kind of blue," and Tracy looked up from his hands and smiled shyly, but Ringo continued to bite his lip and look down.

"Will you look at him?" Ruby said. "Ain't he cute?"

"Come on, Ruby. I ain't in the mood," Ringo said, looking up. His face was still very gentle.

"Is you sad, baby?" she said, going over and putting her hand on his cheek.

"I all right," Ringo said.

"I just don't know what I'm gonna do with you," Ruby said.

Tracy stood up and stretched and yawned, and then

sat down again. He was smiling sleepily. "Boy, that laughing take a lot out of me," he said.

Billy said he guessed it was time he went home, and we all got up and walked slowly toward the door, with Ruby leading the way. Outside, it was foggy and still raining, though it had let up some. Billy came out and locked the door from the outside, and then we all walked up the street. I said I'd go with them a while and get the bus at the stop farther on.

"Well, we certainly glad you is gonna stay with us a while longer," Ruby said, smiling. She took my arm and Ringo's arm.

Tracy walked on ahead with Billy. Billy was wearing a neatly fitting raincoat, and as he walked, very erect and relaxed, he seemed much younger than he did in the grocery store. Tracy walked slouching forward. He was slightly pigeon-toed. "Look at Billy," Ruby said. "He look like a little boy with a big bear."

"Maybe we is them bears," Ringo said to me, looking across Ruby, "and, John, you is Goldilocks." Then he began to laugh very hard by himself.

"Aw, you ain't funny, Ringo," Ruby said, squeezing my arm. "You just ain't funny."

As we approached my bus stop, Ruby told me to take care of myself. "I hope you remember us," she said.

She called to Tracy and Billy to come back and say goodbye to me. They turned around and looked surprised, and then they walked back.

"Look, if you ever sick again," Ringo said, "you come on back and see us."

"Aw, shut up, Ringo," Ruby said. "He don't have to be sick to come back and see us. Right?" She put her arm around my shoulder as I shook hands with Ringo. "He talk like we is some hospital or something," she said.

"Aw, Ruby, you take everything I say and twist it," Ringo said. "Look, John, don't mind nothing I done."

I told Ringo he hadn't done anything.

"You lucky he ain't had more time," Billy said. "He can do some things."

I shook hands with Billy and thanked him for everything. Then Tracy stuck out his big hand. "So long, John," he said. "It been nice knowing you."

The bus was coming down the street rather slowly, because of the fog. When it pulled in, I picked up my suitcase and said goodbye again.

"Goodbye, honey!" Ruby yelled. "Take it easy."

Billy gave a serious little wave, and as I stepped into the bus, Ringo yelled, "I hope the bus break down!" and Ruby hit him on the head with her pocketbook. I heard Ringo say that he had said it for luck, and Ruby told him that she had also hit him for luck. I went to the back of the bus and waved to them from the rear window, and the fog closed in and covered them, and I couldn't see them any more.

Baltimore

ONCE, on a rainy fall evening in Washington, I nearly got into a fight with a squat, round-faced Negro named Ringo Brown, a former professional middleweight fighter, outside a grocery store called Billy's. Ringo started an argument with me and told me to get ready to fight. But there was no fight. After I raised my hands, my left slightly forward, Ringo just laughed and started to kid around. The only reason I ever met Ringo was that I had gone down to Washington from New York to see my family, and on the way home from the station, going through a Negro neighborhood, I had to get off the bus because I felt sick. Ringo just took it on himself to make me feel better. We boxed out in the rain for a while—he wanted to give me some instruction—and I told him to leave me the hell alone because he was making me sicker. "I help you out, John," Ringo said, and he nearly ruined me. After a lot of maneuvering, he finally grabbed my suitcase while I was waiting for another bus, and ran into Billy's with it. I followed him inside. Fortunately, I got to know Billy, the Negro owner. Billy took care of me. He fixed me hot tea and he gave me moral support, and he tried to keep Ringo away from me. I met two other Negroes in the grocery store: Ruby Longstreet, a big-boned, good-looking mocha-brown woman, and Tracy James, a very large man, who was a former heavyweight fighter. We sat around and talked while I dried out, and Billy gave me Coca-Cola syrup in a paper cup. I got to know them. We had a good time and laughed a lot, and when I was finally able to make it they all walked me to the bus. "Goodbye, honey!" Ruby yelled, when I got on the bus. "Take it easy."

When I got back to New York, I wrote Billy a letter, thanking him for everything and sending my regards to Ruby, Tracy, and Ringo. I also sent him an electric hot plate, which I thought he could use at the grocery store. He already had one, but it was falling apart. Billy replied a few weeks later, thanking me for the hot plate and extending a special invitation. Tracy was going to have a birthday party, and they all wanted me to come down for it. They were going to have the party in the grocery store, starting at eight o'clock at night, and, if I could come, there would just be the five of us. He was going to cook some clam chowder on the hot plate, and after dinner there would be a special surprise. Billy said that Ringo missed me, as Ringo had had a lot of fun helping me out. He said that Ringo wanted him to tell me that he, Ringo, thought I was all right for a white man. Ruby sent her love, and Tracy asked me to please come down for his party. At the end of Billy's letter there was a note from Ringo, scrawled in pencil: "Charlie White Man (smile) come on down to Washington. yr. *friend* (Smile!) Ringo."

Billy's letter arrived when I was sick with the flu, but

I hoped to be better in time for the party, three days later, on a Saturday night. I took good care of myself, and when I got on the train for Washington, with a birthday cake for Tracy, I had only a slight cold.

THERE WAS a sign on Billy's door, saying "Closed," and a ripped shade had been pulled down covering the display window from the inside. I tried the door. It was unlocked, and I went on in. They were all there, all dressed up. Billy, a slim and fairly small, light-skinned Negro, was wearing a blue suit, a white shirt, and a solid-blue tie. He looked very dapper. He had looked dapper, though, even in his white apron. Tracy, a big, dark-brown man about six feet four and two hundred and fifty pounds, was wearing a brown suit that was too small for him. It looked as if it had shrunk. The edges of his jacket sleeves were about three inches above the frayed cuffs of his blue shirt, which was frayed also at the collar. He wore a brown-and-red tie of uncertain design, ripped down the center, the white inner lining puffing through. Tracy was sitting on a small packing case, his hands folded across his lap, smiling shyly. Ruby was dancing around in a flaming red dress with an enormous bow in the back and clapping her hands. She was moving very well, looking beautiful, hefty, and solid. Ringo was right behind her. He was smiling, with his eyes closed and arms out, and vibrating, in an old gray jacket too long for him and ripped out at the elbows, a faded blue work shirt, and a dark-red bandanna that was tied around his neck. On his head was the porkpie hat he had worn when I had first met him in the rain almost a month before. Gone were the fatigue jacket and ripped shoes, though. His shoes now were a carefully polished pair of summer brown-and-whites. His pants were dark blue and had a crease in them, and this time he was wearing socks.

When I walked in, Ringo was the first to see me. "Hey, John," he said, running at me. "You come *down!*"

"Hi, honey," Ruby said, smiling and waving.

Tracy waved a big hand and smiled, and Billy came over and shook hands with me. Then Ringo gave me a big bear hug, and I had to raise the cake above my head to keep it from being crushed.

"What you got in that box, John?" Ringo asked, jumping back and then moving in with feints to my body and head.

"Nothing for you, Ringo," I said, winking at Billy, who went over to the door and locked it.

"Hey, John," Ringo said, frowning. "There is a big cockroach going up your pants."

I looked at my pants and saw there was no cockroach. At the same moment, Ringo lunged for the box. I looked up in time to bump heads with him. I dropped the cake, and Ringo, in regaining his balance, stepped on it, his foot going through the box into the center of the seven-layered vanilla cake with "Tracy" written across the top.

There was a low moan from Ruby, and Ringo, looking surprised and a little frightened, pulled his shoe from the cake and hopped backward until he was leaning against the wall. He just looked down at the floor, keeping his cake shoe up in the air.

"Now, look at that. Now, look at that," Ruby said. "Look what that black fool Ringo *done!*"

"I sorry, John," Ringo said, still looking at the floor.

"Who care if you *sorry?*" Ruby yelled, shaking a fist at him. "John don't care."

Ringo took off his shoes and just sat on the floor, his head bowed. Billy picked up what was left of the cake and dropped it in a large cardboard trash box near the counter.

"Forget it, Ringo," I said. "Happy birthday, Tracy."

"Thanks, John," Tracy said, nodding his head and smiling. He pointed to the trash box. "I appreciate it anyhow."

Later on, Billy rolled out a large barrel and placed it in the center of the room; then on top of the barrel he laid a large, square piece of plywood. Ruby spread a white tablecloth over it. Around the makeshift table, Billy set five milk crates for chairs. On the table Ruby put five spoons, five very large tin cups, five cans of beer, an old candy can filled with crackers, five paper napkins, and three red candles, each set in a Pepsi-Cola bottle. "We going to have a *party,* John," Ruby said. Then, looking over at Tracy, she yelled, "Hey, birthday boy!"

"SEE OVER THERE?" Billy said, nodding in the direction of the counter. On the counter, the hot plate I had sent him was supporting a large aluminum pot. "It's cooking just fine, John," Billy said, shaking my hand.

Just before we all sat down at the table, I went to Ringo. He was still sitting on the floor, very quiet, his head bowed. "Come on, Ringo," I said. "Stop sulking."

He didn't say anything.

"It's all right about the cake," I said, kneeling down.

"No, it ain't," Ringo said, shaking his head.

"Accidents happen, Ringo."

"They *always* happens to me."

"You one big accident, Ringo," Billy said.

"It *John's* fault about the cake," Ringo said, suddenly smiling. "He should have *give* it to me." Ringo threw a short jab at my leg. Ruby guffawed.

We all sat down and sang "Happy Birthday" to Tracy, as Ruby lit the candles. Tracy looked down at the table, smiling, seeming a little uncomfortable, a little sad. After we finished singing, we all clapped, and Ruby said, "Well, Tracy, you forty-eight."

"I forty-eight," Tracy said, looking sad.

"That ain't *old*," Ruby said, smiling. "You *young*."

"Yeah, I young all right," Tracy said, looking at Ruby.

She leaned over and kissed him on the cheek. "Honey, you *young*."

"Well, I *feels* young," Tracy said, smiling wide and patting Ruby's hand. Ruby laughed.

"I young, too," Ringo said, looking around.

"You ain't ever been born," Billy said.

Billy brought over the large pot and a ladle. He placed the pot on the floor, next to his chair. "Well, Tracy, we having your favorite food," he said, taking the lid off the pot.

"John," Tracy said, smiling. "I hopes you like clam chowder."

I told Tracy I liked it fine.

"Tracy always have clam chowder on his birthday," Ruby said, passing the cups to Billy.

Billy ladled the chowder into the cups and passed them around, and we started to eat. "You like it, Tracy?" Billy asked, looking worried.

"It fine," Tracy said, nodding. "Just the way I likes it."

"You feel all right, John?" Ruby asked, her forehead wrinkling.

I said I had a little cold.

"Well, we gonna fix you up, John," Ruby said. "You gonna hear something tonight."

"It cure colds," Billy said, nodding seriously.

"Tracy gonna fix us *all* up tonight," Ruby said, putting an arm around Tracy's shoulder.

Tracy smiled.

"Tracy gonna tell a story," Ruby said. "He tell it every five years, on his birthday."

Tracy looked down at his hands.

Billy said that it was a true story, and that this was the surprise he had written me about.

"You the first white man ever heard it, John," Ruby said.

Tracy raised a big hand. "Ruby, maybe John don't *want* to hear it."

"Sure he do," Ruby said. "Right, John?"

I said I did.

"John come all the way down from New York," Billy said, patting me on the back.

We all had a second cup of chowder, and then Tracy had a third. There was nothing else to eat; the chowder was very filling, and there was no need for anything more. While Ruby cleared away the table, removed the cups, and washed them out in a sink in a corner of the room, the rest of us smoked and talked. Ringo asked me if I had done any more boxing since we had worked out in the rain. I told him I hadn't.

"John retire undefeated," Billy said, raising my hand.

Tracy laughed. Ringo, in his socks, began to jump rope without a rope.

"Well, I all finish," Ruby said, coming back to the table. "Sit down, Ringo."

Ringo sat down. Billy walked behind the counter and turned off a small wall light. The room was in semi-darkness, with only the light from the candles on the table. Ruby put her hand on the back of Tracy's neck. "Come on, baby. Let's go," she said.

Tracy looked seriously at the floor for a while—we all waited quietly—and then he smiled and nodded. "O.K., I ready," he said. And then, folding his large hands and leaning forward, he began to tell the story.

"I WAS a soldier stationed at Fort Meade, in the summertime of 1942. I got to say that in those days before I go in the Army, I a heavyweight—I mean a professional and had about forty-two fights, and I guess I pretty good but not getting nowhere. I ain't a top fighter, but I ain't a bad professional, and some people say to me, 'Tracy, you a damn good boy. You gonna be champ,' but I ain't never fooled myself about this champ stuff. So when I go in the Army, I ain't what you call known, though I got this little public here and there, but I ain't no Joe Louis or Billy Conn. On my Army record it say my occupation is pro fighter, and after basic training they got me doing exhibitions before they send me overseas. The exhibitions ain't much—just something to entertain the boys with. Most of the time I don't even go against another pro but against some strong kid who think he can fight. There ain't enough pros to go around. I go against these kids for four, five, maybe six rounds. Maybe they had a few amateur fights or they think they pretty tough. Anyhow, I just carry them. I don't hurt them none, I don't put them down. I hit 'em maybe two, three times a round for my self-respect. So I does my job in the Army, fights these little exhibitions and behaves myself.

"Now, there was this Sergeant Lester Boone. He my top sergeant. Sergeant Boone was a Georgia boy, and he always real nice to me to my face. He say, 'Hi, Tracy. How you feeling?' or 'Tracy, you make a damn fine soldier. You gonna make corporal before you know it,' or sometime, after maybe a fight at Meade, he call me 'Champ.' I guess he all right. He mean well. He just a Georgia boy and can't help himself how he feel about a colored man. It just natural for him, like breathing. 'How you doin', Tracy?' he say to me, but his eyes show he feel a certain way about a Negro.

"Anyhow, while I is in training at Meade, this here general's wife decide to do a good turn for the boys, and she arrange that some society ladies from Baltimore come out on a Sunday afternoon and make a clam chowder and crab-cake meal with some coleslaw for about three companies of soldiers. We all got to be there, because it an order. It don't matter none if you don't like clam chowder and crab cakes. You got to be there. As far as I concern, I don't care much for crab cakes, but I sure do love clam chowder. I got a real weakness for it. When I starts eating it, I can hardly stop. In a way it like a drug or drink habit with me. So I looking forward to the whole thing.

"Well, on Sunday afternoon, about two busloads of these white society ladies come out to Meade, and the buses drive right onto the drill field, where the mess sergeants has set up these tables to put the crab cakes and coleslaw on, and these big pots for them ladies to make the clam chowder in. The ladies brings out these boxes of crab cakes, and some big jars of slaw, and then they gets to work making the clam chowder. They making it all afternoon, and about five o'clock the mess sergeants pass out these big tin cups and plates and spoons and forks, and they say, 'Boys, you eat all you can hold, because you ain't getting nothing else to eat tonight.' Some of them boys kind of upset, because they don't like this food, and they say they rather eat K rations. That was all right with me. The less for them, the more for me.

"I eat clam chowder for about five hours. I line up behind every pot on the field with my tin cup, and them ladies ladle it out to me, and they get to know me real well. They say, 'Soldier, you don't have to feel ashame. You a big man and got to eat,' and 'Soldier, ain't I seen you somewhere before?' They was real nice ladies. They fill my cup, and then I go off a little way and spoon it and drink it down. The sun go down, then it turn dark and they turn on some searchlights to light the field. I think maybe I never been so happy. Them ladies is treating me like a son. 'We never forget you, soldier,' they say to me. I so full I about to explode, but I can't help myself. Well, about nine o'clock the chowder all gone, and the ladies climb into the buses and go away. I go off and lay down and take a little doze, and the next thing I know I is hearing taps. I gets up and looks around, and there ain't nobody on the drill field but me and about ten of them big pots. The lights is out and the boys is back in the barracks, and I really in trouble.

When they have that bed check, they gonna find old Tracy gone. I kinda shaky, and while I going real slow across the drill field, I hear this voice saying 'That you, Tracy?' and Sergeant Boone come up to me, smiling. 'Don't you know, boy, lights is out and they done already played taps?'

"I say, 'Sarge, I really sorry, but I guess I done ate too much and pass out.'

" 'No wonder,' he say. 'You eat enough for a battalion. Everybody talking about you.'

"I say, 'Sarge, I just got a weakness for clam chowder.'

" 'Well, don't worry none this time,' he say. 'Every man entitle to one mistake if it ain't too serious, and you been a good soldier, Tracy, so I ain't gonna put you on report.'

"Well, I thought this little Georgia boy is all right. He all right. I turn in, and the next day I is as good as ever. Sergeant Boone ask me to lead the boys in close-order, and everybody calling me 'Champ,' and not because I is a pro boxer. So life ain't so bad. That night, I sitting by myself writing a letter to my mama, and when I finish the letter I walk over to the orderly room to get a stamp and maybe see if some of the boys hanging around there, but when I get there I see through the window there ain't nobody there except Sergeant Boone. He leaning back in his chair with his legs on the desk, talking on the telephone. He looking like a little bird. I thought I stay outside until he through talking on the phone, because it might be private, and then go in and ask him if he got an extra stamp. I about to walk off a little way so I can't hear what he say, when I hear him say, 'His name is Tracy James.' So I move close to the door to hear what this all about, 'cause it ain't private talk if it about me.

"Sergeant Boone don't say nothing for a while, and then he say, 'This big nigger is just the boy for you. He ain't much.' And then he don't say nothing, and then he say, 'Yeah, that's right. He perfect,' and 'He a pro, but he ain't done much. I seen him fight, and if he go three with Bartel then my mama's an ape,' and then he say, 'Don't you worry none, Barney, 'cause I'm gonna give you two hundred on Bartel, and I ain't throwing my money away this year,' and then he keep telling this Barney not to worry none, 'cause I the boy for Bartel and he ain't never been so sure of nothing in his life, and then he say, 'And I got to tell you one thing, and this important, Barney. This big nigger's crazy for clam chowder. He got a weakness for it. I ain't never seen nothing like it. If you wanna be absolutely sure there ain't gonna be no accident, you just take him out before the fight and fill him full of clam chowder, and when Bartel hit him in the belly with all that chowder, he gonna be one flat nigger.' And then Sergeant Boone laugh and he say, 'That's right. That's right,' and he laugh some more. And then he say he sure he can talk me into fighting Bartel. 'You find a poor nigger,' he say, 'and there ain't nothing he won't do for three hundred dollars.' Now, I don't know why he just can't say I a professional fighter and used to fighting for money and why he can't just leave it go at that. Anyhow, he hung up the phone, and I walk away real quiet and try to think about what I gonna do, and then I decide I go back to the orderly room like nothing happen. Sergeant Boone ain't bother me none. His kind of talk ain't new to me.

"My heart ain't beating fast when I go into the orderly

room, and I feeling pretty good. Sergeant Boone sitting there reading a newspaper. He look up, and at first he look worried, like he afraid I heard what he say, but then I smile, because I don't know why, but I feeling pretty good, and I say, 'Hi, Sarge. How you feeling?' 'Hi, Tracy,' he say, smiling real wide like he never so glad to see anybody in his life. 'I just thinking about you.' He tell me to pull up a chair and sit down, 'cause he want to talk to me about something. I sit down on a chair near the desk and wait. He tap his fingers on the desk and look at me. 'Tracy,' he say, 'what you walking around all by yourself for?' 'I looking for a stamp for this letter,' I say. 'You looking for a stamp, boy?' he say. 'Don't you know the government mail your letters free?' I say, 'I been using stamps all this time, and I guess I done lost plenty of money.' 'Don't you worry about money,' he say. "That's what I want to talk to you about.' But he don't talk about it right off. He ask me who I wrote a letter to, and I say I wrote my mama, and he ask me where she live, and I tell him North Carolina. He say he think it real nice that I write my mama, and he don't think the boys write home enough. They just too busy having a good time and thinking about girls, and we in a tough war, and if you a soldier you ought to be more serious and write to your mama and daddy, and your wife if you married, and tell 'em you all right, 'cause they worry, and I say I agree with him, which I do. He ask me how I like the Army. 'It ain't bad,' I say. 'It could be worse.' He say, 'Tracy, you gonna be a corporal, because you a damn good soldier.' You know, I think he mean it. He mean the other things, but he mean this, too, and I think Sergeant Boone really like me some.

"Then he say to me, 'Tracy, you ever hear of Barney Rand?' I say I ain't, and he say Barney Rand is a big Baltimore promoter and matchmaker, and he was promoting a fight between Young Bartel and some other kid for next week and then this other kid, who was a soldier at Aberdeen, got transferred out, and now Barney Rand is stuck and he gonna have to refund the tickets unless he get a substitute. He say Baltimore nuts over Young Bartel because he won twelve straight fights as a pro, but he frankly don't think Bartel's much. 'Anyhow, Tracy,' he say, 'Barney call and ask if I know any good fighter who can fight substitute, and I say I may know a good fighter right here at Meade, and Barney say, "Well, I hope he a good fighter, because Bartel's manager wants to give the kid good experience and don't want no bum, and Bartel's manager say he gonna take out his boy if I can't get a good fighter." So, Tracy, you can make yourself three hundred dollars next Friday night, and I can fix a pass up for you. What do you say?' I say, 'It's fine with me, Sarge.' He say, 'That's it, Tracy. I'm gonna call Barney tomorrow, and you in for an easy night, because this Bartel done fight a lot of stiffs, and you the first good one that come along.' I say I sure hope he right. He say I don't have to go before no commission or take no physical, because it wartime and I a soldier, who they figure has passed a physical. Sergeant Boone say he gonna send Barney a certificate that I fit. It don't make sense, really, because being in condition as a soldier and a fighter ain't the same thing. 'Don't waste no time training,' Sergeant Boone say. 'Just take it easy and be relax.' He say he gonna let me know more about the fight in a few days, after he know more himself, and I say good night and he say, 'Good night, Tracy, and don't buy no more stamps,' and then he laugh.

"Well, I figure after I left that no boy with twelve fights is gonna make a fool out of me, 'cause by 1942 I done had forty-two pro fights and learned a couple of things, and Bartel ain't gonna take me out unless he a champ on the way, and I ain't worried, but I figure I train a little anyhow, and I figure I do some running and hit the speed bag for timing, which is what I do.

"A couple days later, Sergeant Boone come over to me after some close-order, and he say, 'Tracy, it all set. Bartel's manager say you an O.K. substitute.' I say I glad to hear it. He say, 'It too bad you won't even work up a sweat, but this Bartel ain't much.' 'How I gonna get to Baltimore?' I say. 'On the bus?' 'Hell, no, boy,' he say. 'It all arrange that Barney Rand gonna come out here himself and drive you in right to the arena. All you got to think about is getting in the ring and making a fool out of Bartel.' He say Barney gonna come out to Meade at eight o'clock on the night of the fight and pick me up at the orderly room. 'I be there,' I say. 'You goddam better,' he say, and then he laugh to beat hell.

"Well, during the week, when I get the chance, I do some running and hit the small bag and go to bed early and don't drink no beer or go into Laurel, Maryland, and it seem about three times every day Sergeant Boone say, 'Tracy, how you feeling?' I guess Sergeant Boone really afraid for his money, because on the day I fight he have me on K.P., and I got to get up at four in the morning, and I get the dirty job of cleaning them pots and pans, and Sergeant Boone say he sure sorry he got me on the K.P. the day of the fight, but he say the Army got to go on just the same and it ain't right to give me no special privileges. And I don't say I know he done changed the duty roster, which had give me K.P. on Sunday, two days *after* the fight.

"I work on them pots until three in the afternoon, and then I go over to the gym and get my boxing shoes and some socks and a pair of trunks, and then I go back to the barracks and get my fighting bathrobe with 'Tracy' wrote on the back in white letters, and then I pack my stuff in this little canvas bag and I decide to stretch out on my sack and take a rest. It nice and quiet, because the rest of the boys is out on the firing range. Just when I lay down, Sergeant Boone come in and he say, 'What the hell you think you're doing, Tracy?' I say, 'I just got off K.P., Sarge, and I was gonna take a little rest.' 'You ain't in no rest home,' he say. 'You in the U.S. Army and we in a tough war. You can rest in the car on the way, and in the dressing room.' Then he tell me to go on out and police the area.

"I guess I out there about forty minutes, and when I come back I ask Sergeant Boone if I can go get some chow, because it about five o'clock and I awful hungry. 'While you been gone,' he say, 'I been looking at your rifle, and it don't seem you know how to take care of your weapon.' I say, 'Sarge, I done clean my rifle yesterday, when I come back from the range,' and he say, 'Well, it sure don't pass my inspection, and you ain't gonna get no chow until you clean it proper. You a soldier, boy, and your rifle your best friend.' He say not to leave the barracks until he come back and inspect my rifle personal, and I figure then that I ain't gonna get nothing to eat, and that's how it turn out, because he come back at seven-thirty, and by then the chow hall closed. I ain't touch my rifle, because it clean as it can be, and Sergeant Boone look at it and say, 'See what you can do when you want to?' He say he sorry that he come back so late and that I miss chow, but he had to see the lieutenant, and I can eat on the way into Baltimore. It obvious he don't know nothing about eating before a fight, or maybe it obvious he do, the way things going. I really feeling lousy and not because I don't have nothing to eat but because the way people do, and because it ain't fair, and when you tired and hungry you feel it more, but after a while I all right. You may as well laugh as to cry.

"So, a little later I go over to the orderly room to wait for Barney Rand, and I sit in there with Sergeant Boone and he say, smiling and real friendly again, 'Well, Champ, you in for one easy night,' and 'How you feeling, Tracy?' and 'Ain't no point wishing you luck, 'cause you don't need none,' and stuff like that. I don't say too much and I sit there and conserve myself. I begin to worry a little about the fight and think maybe this boy gonna hurt me bad, the way I feeling. But it don't really matter how I feeling. Even if I feeling strong, I worry some just the same—even if I going in against some boy I know I can take—because when you go in there you never know what gonna happen. The man that say he ain't never afraid is a liar.

"At eight o'clock, Barney Rand come in the orderly room, right on time. Sergeant Boone say, 'Tracy, here is Barney Rand.' Barney Rand look me over and then he shake my hand. He a little guy. He ain't quite a midget —he look like an old jock. Maybe he about sixty years old, and he dress real good, in a dark-blue suit. When he look at me, his eyes get big, and he look a little worried for a second. But then he smile at me and show all this gold in his mouth. 'Tracy, kid,' he say, 'I sure glad to meet you.' But I know that man thinking, Boy, you sure one big nigger, and maybe he thinking he make a mistake. Barney and Sergeant Boone go off a little way and talk real low, and then Sergeant Boone give Barney an envelope, and then they shake hands and Sergeant Boone say real low, but not so I can't hear, 'Everything O.K., if you know what I mean.' And then they shake hands and laugh some. And then Barney say to me, 'You ready, Tracy?' He act like he feeling a little better. 'I ready,' I say, and Sergeant Boone, he slap me on the back and shake my hand, and then me and Barney go out and get in his car—this big Packard—and we start driving to Baltimore.

"We only a half hour away by car, so there ain't no hurry, and Barney drive real slow. He turn on the radio and get some music, and he tap out the rhythm on top of the wheel with one of his hands, and he sing some, but he obvious don't know the words and is making them up, and sometime he don't use words at all but just make sounds, and he don't say nothing to me at first, but he do look at me every so often and smile like he don't want me to think he ain't my pal, and, hell, I smile back, because he sure is some bird, with his skinny little neck, and he a neat little man, and it hard not to like him. After a little while, he say, "Tracy, how come I ain't never heard of you?,' and I don't say in the beginning I used to fight under the name Tracy Holland so my mama don't find out, but then maybe he ain't never heard of

Tracy Holland, neither. 'Well,' I say, 'I ain't never fought none in Maryland, and I ain't fought too much nowhere else, and I ain't done much, which is why you ain't never heard of me.' That seem to make him feel good, and he say, 'Well, Sergeant Boone say you a damn good boy and that you is gonna teach Bartel a few things.' 'I gonna try,' I say. 'Well,' he say, 'I looking forward to seeing you work,' and then he tap it out some more on the steering wheel.

"We drive on awhile, and I just about to ask Barney if we can stop somewhere and get something to eat when he say, 'Tracy, I don't know about you, but I'm hungry and maybe we stop and get a bite.' I say, 'That's O.K. with me, Mr. Rand,' so he pull into some roadside place just outside Baltimore, and he say, 'Tracy, I go in and get some food and we eat it on the way into town.' I tell him that fine with me. He say, 'Now, what you in the mood for?' I say it don't matter much, just a little sandwich is O.K., it don't matter, and he say, 'Well, I don't know about you, but they got some great clam chowder, you can't beat it.' I figure that was coming. 'Yeah, I like clam chowder fine,' I say. I know it wrong to eat so close to a fight, but it better to go in there with a full belly than weak and half starving. They is both wrong, but I figure you is in better shape if you strong than if you weak, and it seem that if I gonna eat, I might as well eat what I love.

"Barney, he come back with enough clam chowder for twenty men, and he say, 'This is my favorite food. I'm gonna take some of it home and have it tomorrow.' I don't say nothing, but just take the lid off a cup and start drinking and spooning it down, and Barney, to make it look right, take a cup and drink a little, too, but then he put the lid back on. 'Well, I got to drive,' he say. 'I guess I just wait until I get to the arena.' By the time he drive the car out to the road, I finish the first cup and is working strong on the second, and Barney looking at me out the corner his eye, which is all lighted up like he is seeing something new. He real excited. By the time we driving through Baltimore, I done finish five cups, because I can't help myself—it ain't hunger no more—and Barney say when I going in the bag for the sixth, 'Tracy, maybe it ain't so good to eat so much before a fight, and besides, some of that chowder belong to me.' I guess he afraid at the rate I'm going there ain't gonna be no fight at all, and that he gonna have a sick man on his hands, and he a little nervous he outsmart himself. So Barney pull over to the side of the road and pick up the bag with them cups of chowder and puts it in the back seat, and he say, 'Now, Tracy, give me the cup that's in your hand,' and I give it to him, and Barney sit there and drink it down himself, and it obvious he don't like it much, but he smile and say it real good. 'How you feeling, Tracy?' Barney say. 'Great,' I say, but when we get out the car in front of the arena I can't stand too good.

"It's a hot night. It's a small arena. Maybe seat a thousand. They some posters up—'James vs. Bartel'—but no pictures. There ain't no promotion, but they don't need none, because Bartel a favorite kid. All they got to do is pass the word. I ask Barney when we walk in the door if anybody in my corner, and he say he gonna put Chalky Haynes in my corner. He say Chalky a damn good colored fighter about forty years ago, and he ask me if I never heard of him. I ain't. He say Chalky in the dressing room waiting for me and I better go in and relax some, and maybe lie down and get my hands taped. The arena pretty well filled when I go in, and some preliminary boys who ain't much is messing around. I goes to the dressing room with Barney, and he say, 'Chalky, this here is Tracy James,' and Chalky, he nod to me, but he don't say nothing. He about sixty-five years old—a little skinny guy. He look some like Barney, except he older and he a colored man. Then Barney leave and Chalky look at me. 'Soldier,' he say, 'you better get out of our uniform and take it easy, 'cause you in for a hard night.' I feeling terrible, and don't feel like doing no fighting. But I know I got to go through with it and that's all there is to it, and it don't matter how bad I'm feeling.

"I get out of my clothes and put on my trunks and then lays down on a table and looks at the ceiling. I don't pay no mind to Chalky, who eyeing me pretty close. I feeling bad all over, and there is only forty minutes before I go in there. Chalky say, 'What in the hell wrong with you, boy?' I say, 'There ain't nothing wrong with me. Just leave me be.' But he don't. He say, 'Look, boy, I a nigger like you, and if you sick, don't go in there. I don't wanna see you get killed. That Bartel liable to kill you if you well, but if you sick he gonna kill you sure!' He really mean it. 'Don't worry about me,' I say. 'I take care of myself.' I don't tell Chalky about the clam chowder, because I ashame of myself and it ain't no use to cry about it. If crying help, I'd cry, but it just make it worse. 'Bartel tough,' Chalky say. 'He hit like a mule kick. He got a good right hand, and you got to stay away from it.' 'O.K.,' I say, but I lay on that table and I ain't thinking of Bartel and the sweat is running down my face and

Bartel's right hand don't mean nothing to me, because when I got a stomach ache that's all I can think about. So Chalky, he tape up my hands, and a little while later Barney come in and say, 'O.K., Tracy, you on.'

"Chalky take a wet sponge and go over my face and he ask me if I cut easy, and I don't say nothing and he say, 'Well, if you cut, I take care of you,' and he put his junk in a little bag, and then I get off the table and put on my blue bathrobe, and I put a towel around my neck. I going through the motions. The pain let up a little, because now I thinking hard about the fight and what I got to do to take care of myself, but when we go out of there, me and Chalky, I still real unsteady on my feet, and I really start to worry some, because when your legs ain't good you got no business going in there. Barney just go to the door of the dressing room with us, and then he say, 'Well, Tracy, good luck,' and he slap me on the back, and then Chalky lead the way up this little ramp, and then we going down the aisle toward the ring, and that crowd start to hoot and laugh at me, and it feel like I never hear them hoots before, like I never fight before. It all seem brand-new, and when I go through the ropes it don't seem like I ever been in the ring before, and it like I see the canvas for the first time. I go right to my corner and don't dance around none, but just sit there and conserve myself and wait for Bartel and sort of look around at the crowd, but don't really see nothing. But when I look down at Chalky I see him real good, and he look real worried and serious, and he climb up on the apron and keep telling me to watch out for the right hand and if I catch one just to stay down and don't get up like no hero. 'You a soldier, boy,' he say. 'You can be a hero in the war.'

"It don't make sense, but, sick and tired as I is, I feeling kind of happy, and the more Chalky say that Bartel one mean bastard the better I feeling. 'Well, here he come,' Chalky say, and we look down the aisle and see Bartel just coming up the ramp, and we see him before the crowd do, and he wearing this bright-red robe, this big blond boy with his hair cut short, and he got wide shoulders that slope some, and I figure he can hit, all right, and then the crowd see him, and the way they whoop and holler you know he the favorite kid, all right. He come down the aisle bobbing and weaving, with about five handlers, and they is all looking real confident and happy like they is champ, and I feeling strange—real bloated and heavy and tired. But I sit there real quiet, and nobody know how I feel. Bartel come through the ropes and dance around, and he look at me and then he look at his handlers, and he got this little smile on his face, and the whole arena is shaking with noise. Bartel a mean-looking bastard. Young and mean. He look in real good shape. I take off my robe and give it to Chalky. Bartel take his off and sit down in his corner, and then Chalky go over to Bartel's corner and watch them put the gloves on him, and then a couple of Bartel's handlers and the referee come over to my corner, and they put the gloves on me.

"Chalky look up at me through the ropes just before I go out for instructions, and he say, 'Stay away from him. Let him come to you. If he hurt you, boy, stay down. Don't be no dumb nigger.' And, sick and scared as I am, he tickle me, and then I get up and go out to the middle of the ring, and Bartel look at me with this little smile, but I don't meet his look and try to stare him down, because that kid stuff and we gonna be at each other soon enough. So the referee give us instructions and say how he want a good, clean fight, and then me and Bartel touch gloves and go back to our corners, and I look down at Chalky and he took terrible, and then the bell sound and we come out.

"I come out low, in a crouch. I is protecting my gut, which is where all the trouble is. If he hit me there, I through. A crouch ain't my natural style, but nothing natural that night, and Bartel come right after me and I keep low and back off and watch his feet and hands, and right away I see he ain't got no left hand. He don't snap it out but just push me with it, and he want to prop me up for the right hand. He throw his right a few times, but I duck under it and hook to the body. I see he got a lot of power in his right, but it don't worry me none, because he give it away by this little head jerk, and I know right then that the only thing I got to worry about is the crowd, and that I can take that kid out any time I want. It don't matter that I feeling heavy and slow, because Bartel ain't got no experience and he just a big, strong kid who don't know what it all about, and I figure that I got to put him out fast, because I liable to get sick. He ain't smiling any more, and he confused because he can't understand why I ain't easy to hit. So, the next time he gimme that wild right hand I go under it and hook him hard on the ribs, and he drop his hands and I come real fast with a right hand to his jaw and Bartel go down on his side, and then he roll over on his stomach and I go to a corner and listen to the count, and on about five Bartel come up on one knee and he try to get up—he looking real surprised, like a little boy, and he don't look mean no more—but he just fall back and sit there while he counted out with his eyes wide open, and the referee come over and raise my hand, and Chalky climb in the ring and help me into my robe, and he smiling, and he say, 'Oh, man, you sure took care of that sucker!,' and then he say I better move out of there, because I just took out a hero and maybe it ain't safe, but there ain't no trouble. That crowd real quiet, like they ain't sure what happen, and me and Chalky move out down the aisle and make for the ramp.

"By the time we make it back to the dressing room, the crowd is booing and stamping feet. They is mad, all right, and maybe they is mad at me and maybe they is mad at Bartel for letting them down, but they is mad and that's for sure, and while Chalky is taking off the tape I get real sick, and I go into the bathroom, and after I come out I feeling much better and Chalky finish taking off the tape. 'You got him in 1:52,' Chalky say, and then he say that Bartel don't belong in the same ring with me. 'No, he don't,' I say. 'Not yet he don't. He got a lot to learn.' Chalky ask me where I learn to fight so good, and I say I ain't that good, I ain't no champ, but I done had plenty experience and knows how to take care of myself. You can teach a green kid, but he got to get his own experience. I don't tell Chalky about how dumb I is about clam chowder, because I ashame of myself. But I guess even an experienced man got his weakness and is foolish sometime.

"I go in and take a shower, and when I come out

Chalky ain't there, and I get dressed and pack my bag and sit around and smoke a cigarette and waits for Barney to come in with my money, and then Chalky, he come in looking worried, and he say, 'Tracy, is your name Holland or James?' And I say my name is James but I used to fight under Holland, and Chalky say that Lou Clark, Bartel's manager, say he remember me and seen me fight on a card in Kansas City in 1939, and I say that he is right, because I fight Levi Collins in Kansas City and got a split decision. Chalky say that Clark say Barney misrepresent and put his boy in over his head, and that he gonna take it to court and fix it so that Barney never promote nothing again, and Barney say that he figure me to be a soft touch for Bartel, and to prove it he say he bet five hundred dollars on Bartel to take me out inside of three, and Clark say that Barney gonna lose more than money when he get through with him and that he gonna lose his promoter and matchmaking license, and Barney, he shake his fist in Clark's face and say that he got plenty of friends and that he gonna see to it that Bartel, or no fighter that Clark represent, ever gonna fight in Baltimore again, and Clark say that Barney know what he can do with Baltimore, and that it just a hick town and Barney a hick promoter, and all the time Bartel sitting real quiet on a chair and looking at his hands like he know he all washed up, and Clark tell him to get up because they in a room with a cheap crook, and then Clark and Bartel go on out.

"Chalky say that Barney plenty mad and that maybe I ought to clear out, but I tell Chalky I ain't going nowhere until I get my three hundred dollars, because I a professional fighter and don't fight for no charity and I ain't done nothing wrong. Chalky say that may be, but Barney mad all the same and there gonna be some trouble. I say if there gonna be trouble I ain't gonna start it, I just want what's coming to me, and Chalky say he with me, but I better watch out. Then, while we talking it over Barney come in and he is all red and burning up. 'What you trying to pull?' he say, and he shake his fist in my face. 'I ain't trying to pull nothing,' I say. 'The hell you say,' Barney say. 'Look here, Barney,' I say, 'you just give me my money and I going back to Meade.' 'You ain't getting no money, boy!' he say. 'We is holding up your purse.' 'You ain't got no right to stop my purse,' I say. And Barney say, 'Why, you black bastard, don't tell me I ain't got no right. You the one ain't got no right. We ain't signed no contract.' And Chalky say, 'Mr. Rand, don't go calling him names like that. Don't you call him no black bastard,' and I tell Chalky to take it easy, and that I gonna handle this my own way. I tell Barney to watch what he call me, and I is getting a little hot because he is hurting my feelings, and then he say, 'No black bastard gonna make a fool out of me.' 'Why, you little runt,' I say, 'you done make a fool out of yourself.' 'The hell you say,' he say, and I tell Barney that I ain't look to fight Young Bartel, and that I fight substitute because Sergeant Boone ask me, and I can't help if he and Boone think I is a soft touch, and as far as I can see he and Boone done outsmart themselves. And then Barney say, 'Boy, you done outsmart yourself, because you ain't getting no money.' 'I know what you and Boone up to,' I say. 'He tire me out all day at camp, and you try to get me sick on chowder, and now, after all that, you mean to say you ain't gonna give me no money?' 'That's right,' he say. 'You ain't getting a nickel.' I start to go at him, because I is real hot, but Chalky come over and grab onto me and Barney jump up and down and say, 'You lay a hand on me and you be in a Baltimore jail the rest of your natural life,' and Chalky pull me away and talk real quiet to me, and he say if I hit a white man in Baltimore it just as bad as hitting one in Mobile, and it even worse, since I is a fighter, and this tickle me and I tell Chalky I ain't gonna hit Barney but just shake my money out of him, and I is O.K. again, and smiling and relax. But Barney, he is still plenty hot and is jumping around, and he say that I misrepresent and maybe now he is ruin as a promoter and matchmaker.

" 'You say your name James, but it Holland,' he say, and I say that Holland just my fight name, and since I ain't no famous fighter it don't matter none and he know it and he just using that as an excuse not to pay me, and then he say, 'Boy, you ruin me. That an excuse, all right.' 'You ruin yourself,' I say, and then so help me God he comes at me—he got a lot of nerve—and take a swing, but I catch his little fist and I hold it, and then he swing the left hand and I catch that, too, and I is holding both his hands, and then I mean to tell you he kick me in the shin, and then Chalky come over and grab Barney by the arms and pull him away. 'Mr. Rand,' he say, 'there ain't no cause for that.' 'You fired!' Barney say to him, and Chalky so surprised he let go Barney's arms and back away, and I walk up to Barney and say, 'Barney, you is your own worst enemy,' and he say he don't want no black bastard to preach to him, and he tell me and Chalky to get out, and I tell him I going to court for that money because I earned it, and he say, 'Boy, you a soldier and we in a war and you don't have any time or money for no court,' and he is right, and I know it, and Chalky say, 'Come on, Tracy, let's go,' and I pick up my bag. I is feeling so disgusted I can't think of nothing to say, but when we get to the door I turn around and look at Barney, and he real red in the face and shaking and twitching and he is a sorrowful sight, and he say, 'Now, you get out 'fore I lose my temper,' and me and Chalky look at one another and we tickle right through, and we start to laugh and we can't stop, and Barney come at us and say, 'Don't you niggers laugh at me. You can drop dead,' and just then, sweet Jesus, he grab at his chest and make this terrible face and keel over and lay on the floor and groan, and his breath real short. Chalky say Barney done had a heart attack, and that he gonna go for a phone and call an ambulance and I should stay in the room with Barney.

"So Chalky go for the phone, and I get a sponge out of Chalky's bag and wet it, and I kneel down near Barney and put the sponge on his forehead, and I say, 'Barney, you gonna be all right. Don't worry about nothing,' and he look up at me, and his eyes real scared, and he try to say something to me but he can't get it out, and I tell him to be real quiet and to take it easy, and I unbutton his collar and I tell you I feel real sorry for that poor little sucker. He look pitiful, like he know he gonna go any minute, and I wished I done had some whiskey with me, because that always good for a man with a bad heart, but I don't have no whiskey and got to be content with using the sponge, which don't help Barney none, but it comfort me.

"Then Chalky come back from the phone and he say, 'Don't you worry none, Mr. Rand. They on the way,' and Barney, he don't say nothing—just lays stretched out looking like a little jock who fall off a horse, and he look so scared. He got tears in his eyes, and I think maybe he ain't scared at all but just mad he can't say nothing mean to me. But I figure maybe he just got a little time left and I don't want it on my mind that I done worried a man out of this world, and so I says to him, 'Barney, I ain't gonna argue about my purse. You can have it. It's yours,' and I tell him I just gonna figure this fight a little workout for me. 'Don't you worry none about me making trouble,' I say. 'You just rest easy.' But Barney look at me like he don't believe me, and Chalky say, 'Tracy ain't gonna make no trouble, Mr. Rand. That's a fact,' and Barney just lays there like he can't understand and I tell you we is plenty scared.

"So then, about ten minutes later, these boys from the ambulance come in with a stretcher and this oxygen machine, and they gives Barney some of this oxygen, and then they lift him on the stretcher and carry him out to the ambulance. Me and Chalky go on out to the ambulance, and we rides in it to the hospital, and them ambulance boys ask me and Chalky a lot of questions, because they say they got to make out a report on what happen. We just say part of the truth—that Barney get real mad and excited about one of the fights and then he just keel over—but we don't go into no details about no argument, because that just make everybody look bad, and it don't really matter none nohow, and we ask them ambulance boys how Barney doing, and they say maybe he gonna pull through and maybe he ain't, but he a sick man and we just got to wait and see.

"When we gets to the hospital, they take old Barney on in and we follows right behind, and Barney all covered up with a blanket and he look more dead than alive. He look kind of gray, and his eyes don't say nothing one way or another. Them ambulance boys say they gonna take Barney to this room and put him in an oxygen tent. They say we got to wait outside in this waiting room, if we feel like sticking around, and Chalky say, 'Sure, we sticking around, what you think?'

"So we sits there and smokes, and Chalky talk some about Barney, and how he ain't really a bad guy but he got kind of a hot temper. Chalky say he know Barney about fifteen years and Barney been real good to him, all things considered, and I say, 'Well, Chalky, he done fired you,' and Chalky say, 'Aw, hell, that ain't nothing new. It don't mean nothing.' We sit there for something like three hours, and about two in the morning this doctor come out and he say, 'Boys, I think he gonna be all right.' He say you can't be certain with heart attacks, and maybe they got to wait a few days to be sure, but as far as he is concern there ain't nothing much to worry about and Barney gonna live a while yet if he take care of himself and keep cool. In that case, I figure he ain't got much time. If it ain't today, then it tomorrow. But me and Chalky breathe easy. In a way, I feel I nearly kill a man, but deep down I know Barney nearly kill himself. I glad he is alive, because I like Barney. I guess some men just easy to like and it don't matter what they do. Chalky ask the doctor if Barney got any message for us, and the doctor say whichever one is Chalky is suppose to go to Barney's hotel and get his pajamas, bathrobe, and slippers and to buy him a toothbrush and he pay it back, and I say, "Chalky, maybe you better check Barney out of the hotel if he gonna be here awhile,' but Chalky say that Barney live in this hotel all year round and he paid up six months in advance. So me and Chalky shake hands with the doctor and go on out, and when we gets on the street Chalky say, 'I got a car. I drive you back to Meade,' and we walk back to the arena, which take about forty minutes, and we gets in Chalky's old Dodge car and drive on back to Meade.

"I is real tired. It been a long day, and on the way back I is all mixed up and it don't seem like nothing is real, and it seem like a dream, but when I think about the three hundred dollars it seem real all right, and I plenty disgusted about my money. And Chalky say he don't blame me and I got a right to be disgusted, but he say it only money and I is better off than Barney, laying in that hospital, and I say he is right but that ain't the point. 'Maybe he send you the money someday,' Chalky say, but I tell Chalky I don't want the money now, because I done give it away to a dying man and I ain't going back on my word. But I is just disgusted about everything. When we gets to Meade, Chalky stop the car at the gate, and he say, 'Tracy, you take it easy, now,' and I say, 'So long, Chalky, I look you up in Baltimore sometime,' and I slip him five for bringing me back to Meade, and he say he don't want no money, and I keep telling him to take it, and finally he say, 'I take it. Now you out three hundred and five bucks,' and we laugh some. Might as well.

"I figure what's coming with Boone, and I ain't wrong. He waiting for me outside the barracks, and right away I see he know all about the fight and that he ain't a winner, but he don't say one word about the fight. 'Tracy,' he say, 'what you think you is, some privilege character?' and I say, 'Sarge, I don't rightly know what you mean,' and he say, 'Your pass good until one o'clock in the morning, and it now going on four,' and I pull out my pass and look at it and there ain't no time on it, and I tell Sergeant Boone I figure I just got to get back before reveille, and he say he don't put no time on the pass but he say he *tell* me I got to be back before one, and I say I don't remember him telling me that, and he say, 'Tracy, you calling me a liar?' and I say I ain't calling him no liar but I don't remember, and he say that ain't no excuse and that maybe I'm gonna get a summary court—not just for coming back late but for being disrespectful to a noncommission officer.

"After that, I don't say nothing more about the pass, but I tell Sergeant Boone that Barney done had a heart attack and I was at the hospital and that is why I come back so late. He look real serious and concern, and he ask how bad it is, and I tell him what the doctor say, and he don't say nothing for a minute, and then he say, 'No wonder he done have a heart attack!' and then he tell me that I'm still in plenty trouble, because I got my obligation to the U.S. Army and nobody else, but he seem sorry to hear about Barney. He don't give me no summary court, but put me on K.P. for two weeks solid, and he restrict me to camp right up to the time we ship out for overseas, and so I never did get back to Baltimore before I went over, and I ain't never seen Barney Rand or Chalky again, though I hear that Barney still jumping around Baltimore. I don't know what become of Chalky, and I suppose he gone. He ain't in his prime twenty years ago."

Mary Jane

WHEN THEY ARRIVED in New York, coming up from Washington on a Monday, Stedman had missed the Lincoln Tunnel exit and had driven to the George Washington Bridge, because he had gotten in a furious argument with her. "You know damn well—you know damn well I can't stand it—just so contrary and unpleasant, and you take such positive delight in upsetting me—"

Mary Jane began to breathe in gasps, turned red, and then began to laugh hysterically, feeling frightened and hating herself. Stedman missed the tunnel, and came into New York, crossing the Hudson at the George Washington Bridge, and then he made the wrong turn, and they found themselves on the way to Connecticut. It was Mary Jane's twenty-first birthday.

Lately, she always felt slightly delirious in his company; it was as though her impression of him, even as she looked at him, kept shifting and changing, perhaps four or five times in the space of a minute.

"Oh, Stedman, you're an awful driver. You're always getting lost, lost, lost, lost."

As they drove down the drive toward the city, Stedman, in spite of her, began to get excited.

"Look at the Hudson. Have you ever seen anything so beautiful? Now I mean it. Virginia or Maryland can't compare to New York. I mean scenically—"

"Are you kidding, Stedman?" she said, yawning. "Everybody knows the Hudson's a sewer, and New York State can't compare to Virginia. Lord, you're really crazy. Really—oh, you just make me so tired. How you rant on. Would you mind putting out that awful intellectual pipe or at *least* open a window?" She lit a cigarette, and looked out at the late afternoon sunlight on the water. It really was nice, she thought, but it couldn't compare to Virginia, or even Maryland for that matter.

"I can hardly breathe, Stedman," she said, as they entered traffic on Fifty-seventh Street. "It's all just sound and fury and bad air." She was sorry she had come, but Stedman, feeling their marriage was in crisis, thought they needed a little trip, and he had gone to a great deal of trouble to get a week off, beginning on her birthday, and arrange for theater tickets and so forth. But she had put her foot down on meeting any of Stedman's law school friends. He had promised not to call them, but she was afraid accidents could always happen, and they just might run into them on the street. They were so *dreary,* she thought, and their wives were even worse, thinking they were so advanced and going on about plays they had seen and books they had read, like lecturers. And they were all in causes. They were all just so gross, like Stedman, she thought, all messed up in causes, and yet not having any real honor, or kindness or *quality.* They just wanted so desperately to appear literate and informed, and she'd be damned if she'd spend any time in the company of that awful, horrid bitch, Ellen, the wife of Stedman's law school roommate, who found her so *amusing*. Once when they had walked down Fifth Avenue, Ellen kept saying, "Mary Jane, you walk so *slow*. Why do you keep hanging back, honey chile?" in what she, Ellen, thought was a fine imitation of a Southern accent, and they had all joined in, and Mary Jane had said, "I don't like to sprint. I like to walk." She always walked too slow for New York but not for Washington, where she lived, or Roanoke, where she was from. They had all, almost right from the start, found it so amusing that she was Southern.

Stedman had put out his pipe, and while driving through the heavy crosstown traffic, looked over at her occasionally. She would meet his glance with a face devoid of expression, then, suddenly dropping her mouth open, she would squint, mimicking his expression when he was without his glasses.

"You're not very funny, Mary Jane. Really," he said.

SHE REMEMBERED the last time she was in New York, to help Stedman celebrate his tenth class reunion at the Columbia Law School. It had been the year before, and it was the first reunion Stedman had attended since his graduation. It was then she had met many of Stedman's classmates and their wives for the first time (she had already entertained some of them in Washington where they, like Stedman, worked for the Department of Justice or with some agency). Sitting in the car, she had to smile when she thought of the reunion, and she looked quickly at Stedman with tenderness, remembering how pathetic and sweet he had been, worrying about whether he had aged. The night before the festivities, they had arrived in New York on the train and checked right in to the New Yorker Hotel across from Pennsylvania Station so Stedman could get a good night's sleep. Mary Jane suddenly snorted and covered her face with her hands, when she remembered how at the reunion cocktail party she was with him when they overheard a blond, curly-haired classmate named Carter Blakewell say, "My God, have you seen Stedman Greer? He looks old." It had been so awful, so ridiculous. Stedman became so upset he had to leave the room, and she followed him out, trying to console him as best she could. She told him that some people always look more *mature* than their contemporaries. "Sted, I bet you looked fifteen when you were ten," she had said, and he had suddenly agreed, looking hopeful. "You look just fine, Sted," she had told him. "Really. Just fit and fine—and young enough for me." They had gone back in to the reunion, where Stedman had enjoyed himself, feeling very proud of Mary Jane who he felt was the most attractive and charming girl there. Actually, she thought, it wasn't so bad, except for the wives and all the talk about political action and "ideas" that took place later on, all the talk about the backward South and its backward people. It was the beginning of the end of their marriage. She felt that Stedman was as ashamed of her during the discussions as he had been proud earlier at the cocktail party, because her accent was Southern and she'd had a perplexed expression on her face, and later on she had said something vaguely rude to a former professor of Stedman's while they were all having dinner in a Chinese restaurant. The professor, a short man in his fifties, winking conspiratorially at Stedman and the group, had taken her hand and said, "I have a story that you might appreciate." He looked briefly at Stedman, who smiled. "This Negro and his wife attended a night club where these white dancers were performing their act, and this Negro turned to his wife and said, 'My, those white boys sure have a fine sense of rhythm.'" Everybody laughed. Mary Jane remained impassive and a little stiff, and when the laughter died down, the professor smiled at her and said, "You don't think it's funny?"

"No. And it's just all wrong and stale," Mary Jane said, flushing. "Negroes *do* really have a better sense of rhythm than whites, and they can also run faster generally because of something about their tendon—its shorter or something—and besides, why do you want to make everybody the same? It's all just so boring—" She had lit a cigarette and tried not to look at anyone. Mary Jane remembered that Stedman was so embarrassed that he could hardly eat his won ton soup, four wives just looked at her with positive hatred, and the professor, after taking her hand and patting it, began to talk about something else.

THEY DROVE to the Plaza Hotel, where they had reservations for a large room overlooking Central Park. The Plaza was Stedman's idea. He wanted to create the proper mood for reconciliation, and he imagined the hotel might appeal to Mary Jane's sense of tradition and the past.

When they pulled up, under the Plaza marquee, Mary Jane jumped out of the car, without waiting for the doorman or Stedman, who had also quickly gotten out, to open the door for her. She wore a camel's-hair coat with a belt in the back. She had a graceful body and gray eyes, with a green kerchief over long brown hair, and her skin was rosy and golden. Stedman thought that to look at her then, one could hardly know how unbelievably temperamental and touchy she was; sometimes she terrified him, particularly lately, with her quick temper and sharp tongue, but there in the afternoon sunlight, he was so desperately in love with her, so agonized at the thought of losing her, that he did not hear the doorman or the bellboy asking him what he wished done with the bags and the car. Mary Jane, her hands in the pockets of her coat, quickly went up the steps and in through the revolving door. She had lovely, long legs, was very well-co-ordinated and moved beautifully, Stedman thought.

He gave instructions to the doorman that his red Thunderbird (which Mary Jane had described as "very gross, Stedman, about par for you") should be parked in the hotel garage, and he told the bellboy to take the bags in and he would meet him at the desk.

He stood, looking a little sad and lost, and watched some people, mainly young couples, sitting in the sunlight near the fountain in the plaza, and he thought it was really quite simple to be happy. He began to nod, affirming the thought, and he stood there for some time, slightly round-shouldered and overweight, his face a bit puffy. He took off his glasses and wiped his eyes, and then he felt his hair. It was getting thinner, he thought.

Up in the room, Mary Jane immediately kicked off her shoes and lay down on the bed, still wearing her coat.

She sneezed and put a hand to her forehead. She wasn't feeling very well.

"Mary Jane, have you seen this view?" Stedman said, by the window. "It's just fantastic. Come on and look."

She didn't say anything. He was always telling her to look at something—sunsets, full moons, clouds—and it irritated her. He was always killing her aesthetic pleasure by pointing something out and giving her a description. "You're really killing it for me, Stedman. Do you know that?" she said. She felt a little warm, and thought she was getting sick.

"Oh, come on," Stedman said, putting his pipe in his mouth. "The sun's going down and you won't be able to see—"

"I'll see it tomorrow, Stedman."

"Not in this light."

"Oh, leave me alone."

Looking hurt, Stedman lit his pipe and continued looking at the view of Central Park, which, from the fifteenth floor, enabled him to see the entire area, all the way up to 110th Street. He watched the skaters and thought it was a beautiful scene, the figures sliding around the white rink, with the trees and open areas giving it a strange and wonderful quality, particularly in the twilight. He was about to say something more to Mary Jane about coming to the window, about how the skaters looked, but he thought better of it. Sheepishly he turned and looked at her, hoping that something pleasant and friendly might pass between them, but she was not looking at him; she lay on the bed, on her side, her eyes closed. He walked over to the bed and sat down hesitantly on the edge and placed a hand on her shoulder. He asked her how she was feeling. She didn't say anything, and he said, "Jesus, you're looking so beautiful. I feel like making love." Abruptly she sat up. "Stedman," she said. "I don't feel like making love—not with you. Now you just go read the newspaper."

Her face was very serene, with only the faintest trace of anger around her mouth; her eyes were large and gray and lively, and Stedman thought she was probably thinking of something awful to say to him. Feeling humiliated, he got up, and, with his hands behind his back and his pipe in his mouth, he withdrew into the bathroom and turned on the faucet, standing there for what seemed like a long time, in an effort to regain his composure.

Mary Jane lay with her eyes closed, trying to understand why she had ever married him, trying to remember the strange crazy appeal he had had for her when he had come down to Roanoke two years before on an antitrust case for the Justice Department. Stedman had come down to see her father who was a lawyer representing a firm that Stedman claimed was "conspiring to restrain trade," and her father, after they'd had a discussion in his office, had invited Stedman to come home for dinner. It was all very fine, she remembered. Stedman was an enormous hit. He was in turn shy, painfully shy, wildly outspoken, laughing, solemn and deliberate, pompous and ridiculous—and he had a way of stopping in the middle of a sentence suddenly, as though he feared he had gone too far. She had thought him very amusing, honest and basically good, even sexually attractive, and he'd had all these ideas about civil rights, about justice and equal rights for all, that appealed to her, and she loved the sincerity of his convictions and the fact that he was interested in the world and that he thought about things. It was all so enormously different from her own trivial personal preoccupations and from the normal concerns of her own family. They had all found Stedman amusing and wrong in his ideas, and had chided him for not really understanding Virginia or the problem with the Negroes—after all, he was from Buffalo, N.Y., and so he was just naturally confused—but they had liked him and treated him warmly and with an honest affection that amazed Stedman, particularly since they had known him for just a few hours. Stedman had told Mary Jane that her family—her mother and father, and her seventeen-year-old brother, Raleigh—was the most charming group of people he had ever had the good fortune to meet, and that she was the loveliest girl he had ever known. He had kept coming back down to Roanoke on official business regarding the antitrust case, and he was still making the trip down from Washington two months after the case had been dropped. In late summer, he asked her to marry him, and she accepted. Her parents did not offer much resistance, though her mother had reminded her that Stedman was from Buffalo, that his ideas and background were different from their own, but, conceding that times were changing, that Mary Jane was in love with him, they gave their blessing and consent.

Stedman had not wanted a large, formal wedding. His own family was small. His father, a former musicologist at the University of Buffalo, had died three years before. An older brother, Ardman, with whom he had never been close, was living in San Francisco, and would never come East for the wedding anyway. He had never been friendly toward any of his aunts or uncles or cousins. Only his mother and a few college and law school friends might have attended on his side. He had just wanted to slip away and get married. And besides, it would have been awkward and embarrassing for his mother to have come down to Roanoke to meet Mary Jane's family, particularly in light of the one meeting between Mary Jane and his mother, which had been disastrous. Mary Jane thought of the meeting. Before they'd informed her parents of their desire to get married, she had gone up to Washington to meet Stedman's mother, who had come down from Buffalo. Lying on the bed at the Plaza, Mary Jane thought of her. Oh, that old biddy, she thought. That dried-up old bitch. Stedman's mother had been very critical of her, in manner and tone. She had the gall to *condescend,* Mary Jane thought, in her awful, severe clothes, with her awful pinched face. Oh, God, what a torment that was, she thought, to spend three hours in the company of that tiresome, cold, self-righteous woman, and she's just responsible for all of Stedman's problems, and the hell with her. Mary Jane thought of Stedman's mother as a Professional Moralist, involved in causes as an excuse to express hatred toward people that would be difficult to express otherwise. She doesn't give a good goddam about justice, Mary Jane thought, and if she does, who in the hell wants her justice, that old bitch, and she had the gall to ask me, almost right off, without any warm courteous welcome or just an ordinary simple kindly greeting that would certainly be appropriate toward the girl her son was about to marry, to ask what I thought about civil rights and what *I* and *people like me* proposed to *do* about it, and I said, "Oh, I'm going to line my family up against the wall and shoot them. How's that for a start?" and Stedman's mother said, "Don't be flippant with me, young lady," and I was just shaking like a leaf and close to tears (she moved her lips and formed the words, "that old bitch"). She remembered how Stedman had been mortified—it was the first time she sensed that he had been ashamed of her—not because he really cared about his mother, but because he felt that her reply was too emotional, defensive, too typically Southern, and that she had missed the point altogether. "You mean I've got to sign a loyalty oath for your mother? Is that it, Stedman?" she said later. Even before the meeting, Stedman had known how his mother had disapproved of Mary Jane. Earlier she had confided to him on the telephone that she feared that her worst anxieties would be borne out, that Mary Jane would be one of those "awful Southern girls—pretty, but basically stupid and unredeemable." Mary Jane had been prepared for Stedman's mother, for he had admitted that his mother was a little "perplexed" that he had decided to marry a Southern girl, but he had hastily added, "She'll come around when she sees you, Mary Jane, just like everyone else." But she hadn't come around, and Mary Jane all but told Stedman how much she hated her, and Stedman stood around, looking terribly worried and anxious, after they'd all had dinner together—four courses and a lengthy silence, as Mary Jane recalled—in a Washington restaurant. The following day, Stedman's mother had got on the train for Buffalo. He had seen her off, and her last words to him, as he placed her suitcase on the rack above her seat, were, "You're a fool, Stedman. You're out of your mind. She's a little horror, and you'll be very sorry." Six weeks later, Mary Jane and Stedman eloped and were married by a justice of the peace in Elkton, Maryland. Stedman had wanted to move to New York City, which he had grown to love during his Columbia days, but Mary Jane wouldn't go farther north than Washington. She wanted to be able to look across the Potomac and see Virginia, and she truly loved Washington, and they had remained there.

MARY JANE, after falling asleep briefly, awoke to find Stedman placing a blanket over her feet. He was smiling when she opened her eyes; he had changed his clothes and was wearing his new blue suit, a white shirt, and a blue tie with white stripes. The suit was one she had selected for him three weeks before, when he had asked her to come with him out of respect for her taste and judgment, but in truth he wanted her to make the selection to be immune from her criticism. She had accused him in the last year of dressing as he did only to torment her with his "gross appearance."

"How are you feeling?" he said.

She rubbed her eyes and yawned, placing a hand over her mouth. "I had better get dressed," she said, jumping up and taking off her camel's-hair coat. She hung up her coat and then opened her suitcases, hanging up her dresses and a coat of beaver fur, and then placed her underwear and stockings in a bureau drawer, and then, wearing only a half slip and bra, with her blue robe over her arm, took her toothbrush and toothpaste into the bathroom and took a shower. Stedman turned on the television, then turned it off and began to read the newspaper, then suddenly he threw the paper on the floor and sat there looking at his hands. The smile that had lightened his face on seeing Mary Jane awake had disappeared, and he had now that particular expression of confusion and sadness that at different times evoked in Mary Jane feelings of tenderness, of scorn, of impatience, of guilt—depending on her mood. He got up and pulled out his pipe from his coat pocket. Just then Mary Jane came out of the bathroom in her blue bathrobe, and he put his pipe back in his pocket and sat down and picked up the paper from the floor.

Mary Jane didn't feel well. She felt she was coming down with a cold but said nothing to Stedman. She went into the small dressing room, just off her closet, and changed into a simple black dress and put on a string of pearls that her father had given to her for Christmas, put on her shoes, and then quickly sat down at the dressing table in the bedroom and applied her make-up—some pale red-orange lipstick and a little eye shadow, and then she brushed, then combed her hair. Watching her, Stedman wondered how such a lovely, natural, and beautiful girl could have ever wanted to marry him.

They went down to the lobby. It was a little after six o'clock. Stedman had planned a quiet evening of dinner and theater—"without my law school friends or their wives, Mary Jane. We'll do what you want," he had told her in Washington when they had planned the trip—and down in the lobby, Stedman suggested that they go into the Palm Court and have a drink before dinner. It was crowded, and Stedman suddenly felt very excited to be with her in that atmosphere, where everything seemed promising and hopeful again. He wanted to sit in the

Palm Court in his new suit, and Mary Jane looking beautiful.

"Crazy things give you a lift, Stedman," she said, when he told her how he felt about sitting in the Palm Court with her. He had been smiling, but upon seeing her expression, he lost his confidence. "If you must know, Sted, I find the Palm Court very tiresome, and I find it very boring that it gives you a lift, and why can't you just relax?"

"But I feel relaxed in the Palm Court," Stedman said, hurt and defensive.

She felt very nervous and bitchy. She bit her lip.

"Look, Sted, I'm sorry. Let's have a drink here," she said, suddenly. "I mean if that's what you want. No, really, there's nothing wrong with the Palm Court, and if you like it here, why not, Sted, really—I'm sorry."

They had a drink. Mary Jane had a double martini and Stedman ordered a champagne cocktail. Halfway through his drink, his confidence restored, he grinned fatuously and took her hand, and shook his head several times; she knew he was about to make one of his rapturous declarations. Stedman looked around the court, and then he looked at her again and said, "Mary Jane, I love you—I know what you must think of me—but I love you. I love you more now than I did when I married you, and I loved you then. But now—I mean I know everything's going to be all right—and I love you more now, and believe me you've been a wonderful wife—"

She withdrew her hand and lit a cigarette; then she brought her glass to her mouth and looked at him; her gray eyes were slightly misted over. She had expected something ardent—it hadn't really changed anything—

but he looked so vulnerable and so pathetically hopeful, and even a little ridiculously proud in the blue suit she had picked out for him, that she was moved almost beyond belief, and, taking another sip of the martini, she put her glass down very carefully on the round tabletop and said, "That's very sweet, Sted. Really."

They had dinner at a little French restaurant in the East Fifties, and Stedman, who was proud of his ability to read the menu, ordered for her (though she could speak and read French better than he), and he ordered the wine from the steward without failing, as she anticipated, to get into a discussion of vineyards and France. During dinner, Stedman was animated, and, in Mary Jane's view, nearly hysterical, and he kept saying, "We needed a vacation. We had to get off by ourselves," and later on, he said, "My God, you know it's a beautiful world," and all during dinner, during the five courses, Stedman talked, took Mary Jane's hand, kissed her hand, kissed her cheek from time to time, wished her happy birthday, began talking fitfully about his early years in Buffalo and the heavy snows, and everything was so disconnected and incoherent, and he never once, Mary Jane thought, discussed or alluded to one thing that was really at issue between them; he was evading everything as usual, and although she had nearly made up her mind to leave him, she was still impatient with his evasions, with his ability to get everything wrong and create so much confusion. She thought that he was a master of evasion, that he was then being drunkenly evasive, but that he could be evasive by being sober and measured and deliberate as well. Oh, but I haven't been too lucid myself lately, she thought, particularly with Stedman persecuting me all the time. During coffee—after Stedman had lighted a cigar and suggested that they have a cognac—she took his hand and said, "Sted, we better go. We're going to be late for the theater."

"*Madame, tu es tres gentille,*" Stedman said, getting up from his chair and cupping her head between his large hands. "You know how I feel about you, don't you?" he said, suddenly becoming very serious, assuming an almost desperately solemn expression which, in its sudden transition from false gaiety, gave Mary Jane a start. She was beginning to feel somewhat lightheaded and sick, and she thought she had a fever.

"*Au revoir,*" Stedman said, smiling at everyone, and they left the restaurant, stepped out into the cold night where Stedman, half singing and half calling, hailed a cab for the Billy Rose Theatre.

It was very cold in the theater. In the middle of the first act, she said to Stedman, "My God, I'm freezing to death." Stedman whispered that it was terribly cold, and that something must have gone wrong with the heating system. She put her beaver coat around her shoulders, and Stedman placed his own coat over her legs; she slumped down in her seat and closed her eyes, feeling feverish and ill. She sneezed several times, and then a headache began to press down so hard that she was forced to close her eyes and open her mouth. She thought she'd pass out from the pain. She could no longer hear the dialogue, much less see what was happening on stage, and she lost the continuity of the play. By the end of the first act, her teeth were chattering, and Stedman, full of wine, had fallen asleep. She nudged him. People were trying to get by for the intermission break, and

Stedman, looking embarrassed and sleepy, stood up and let them pass.

"Sted, I'm sick. I've got to go back to the hotel. You stay and see the play," she said.

"You don't feel well?" Stedman said, trying to focus on her in the confusion of the intermission. He had a slight hangover, and he felt disoriented. "What's the matter?"

"I'm sick, Stedman. You stay and I'll see you back at the hotel."

"Oh, no. Look, if you're sick—"

All of his elation of the early evening, of the dinner, had passed, and, looking at Mary Jane, her lovely high color gone, her gray eyes in pain and impatience demanding to end the evening that had started out so well, Stedman felt depressed and disheartened, as though in some way he was being punished again for having done something wrong. All the way out of the theater, still half asleep, he tried to understand what he had done, and then felt guilty that he was more concerned with his own conscience than he was with Mary Jane's illness, which he had nearly forgotten about by the time they made their way through the crowded lobby and reached the street.

Mary Jane got right in bed, and Stedman went out to a drugstore and purchased decongestants, aspirin, and a thermometer. When he came back to the room, the lights were on, and she lay on her back, looking at the ceiling.

"How are you feeling?" he said, putting his purchases on the night table.

"Wonderful, Stedman. I have a virus."

He took her temperature. It was 102 degrees F., and he wanted to call a doctor, but Mary Jane said she would be all right in the morning. She took some aspirin with a glass of water that Stedman had brought her from the bathroom, and then she turned out the lamp on the table by her bed, and, without saying goodnight to him, turned over and went to sleep.

Stedman turned off the overhead light, then sat in a chair in a corner of the room, and gradually as his eyes became accustomed to the darkness, he could clearly see Mary Jane sleeping on her side. Her breathing was regular but congested, and she rolled over several times in her sleep, and, moaning slightly, pushed the pillow away, then folded it in her arms, then finally pushed it off the bed. Stedman went over and picked up the pillow and placed it near her head in case she wanted it later in the night. He went back to the chair and continued to watch her. She was so beautiful, he thought, even when she was sick. It amazed him that she was always graceful; he thought that no matter what position she was in, she always looked lovely and in harmony, while he, on the other hand, almost always looked awkward, even under the best conditions. Stedman thought about her wonderful co-ordination. He remembered how easily she beat him at tennis, without hardly trying, and she even beat him playing with her left hand. Stedman was convinced that with her natural ambidextrous talents, she could have been a great tournament player, if she had been at all serious about it. Once she gave him five games and beat him. He was so proud of her—the way she concentrated and went after the ball, tormenting him with lobs and drop shots and fantastic placements down the line—that he had been overcome with admiration and love for her, and he had made some ardent declaration, and Mary Jane said, "Oh, Sted, come on!" And the first time he saw her on a horse, when he visited her in Virginia, he knew that if he lived to be a very old man, he would never see anything more lovely than Mary Jane sitting on a horse, or Mary Jane taking the jumps, or at a fast gallop. She was a beautiful rider. It was all so effortless and natural, and she was so fearless and lovely at the same time. And above all, he thought, she was a fine person, loyal and true and honest, while he was so awful, so gross. She was right about that, he thought. He took out his pipe, placed the stem against his cheek, then put it in his mouth, continuing to sit in the darkness, looking at Mary Jane, who was now in a deep quiet sleep. Stedman leaned back in the chair and closed his eyes. In a few minutes, the pipe fell out of his mouth and on his lap, and he began to snore. He awoke with the dawn light coming through the window, his back aching terribly. He got up and staggered over to his bed and fell down on the spread, and in this way, still in his shoes and clothes, he slept for three more hours.

When Mary Jane first opened her eyes about ten o'clock, her throat was sore, her chest congested, and she ached in her arms and legs. She glanced over at Stedman, who was still stretched out on his bed in the very position he had collapsed onto it—spread-eagled on his face, with his legs hanging extended over the corner. She sighed. She wanted to cover him with a blanket, and she propped herself upon her elbows, in an effort to get out of bed, but she felt too weak and dizzy, and she lay back down on her back. She reached for the thermometer on the night table, shook it down, and placed it in her mouth. Looking over at Stedman again, in his new blue suit all wrinkled, she thought that Sted couldn't even take his coat off, and he's just so sloppy. A few minutes later, she removed the thermometer and noted that her temperature was 100 degrees F., shook the thermometer down weakly, put it on the night table, then lay back down. She felt so weak, and she just hated to feel weak. It unnerved her. She lit a cigarette, but her throat was so sore she immediately put it out. Then she reached for her pillow and threw it onto Stedman's bed, hitting him on the back. "Stedman, wake up," she said, but he didn't move. "Oh, damn you, Stedman, will you *please* get up?" He grunted but remained lying on his face. She picked up the telephone and asked the operator to please ring their room immediately, ten long rings, and hung up. The phone began to ring, and on the eighth ring Stedman opened his eyes and turned over and looked at her. Mary Jane picked up the phone and thanked the operator, and then she looked at Stedman who sat up on the edge of the bed, his head in his hands.

"You're so messy, Stedman," she said. "Do you hear me?"

His face was red and creased from where it had pressed into the bedspread. His eyes were bleary. He stooped over and took off his shoes, and then wriggled his feet.

"I feel awful," he said, shaking his head, then placing the heels of his hands against his temples. "What time is it?"

"It's after ten," Mary Jane said, lying back.

"We better get started," Stedman said, yawning. "The Guggenheim opens around—" Then he looked at her, suddenly remembering that she had been ill. "How are you feeling?" he said, with a slightly guilty look on his face.

"I don't feel so well, Stedman," Mary Jane said, lighting another cigarette. "You'll have to go to the Guggenheim without me."

"Sweetheart," Stedman said. "You shouldn't smoke when you're sick." He shook his head. "Listen, I'm not going anywhere without you. I'll call room service and order you some breakfast, and we'll have breakfast in bed."

Mary Jane said that she wasn't hungry, and that she wasn't having anything in bed with Stedman, and he laughed and tucked in his shirt and picked up the telephone. He ordered two breakfasts of orange juice, bacon and eggs, toast, and coffee.

Mary Jane drank her juice and ate a piece of toast and drank a cup of coffee. Stedman ate her bacon and eggs as well as his own. She marvelled at his appetite. He was always so hungry, she thought, for food, for love, for everything.

"Look," Stedman said. "I'll get the morning papers and some magazines, and we'll just spend a leisurely day in the hotel and maybe tonight you'll feel well enough to go to the theater."

"I'm sick, Stedman," she said, with irritation. "I won't be able to go out tonight."

Looking confused and guilty, Stedman went into the bathroom and splashed some cold water on his face, and he came out holding a towel.

"Mary Jane, it's really no tragedy about the tickets. We'll just let them go. It's no tragedy—"

"Take one of your law school friends," Mary Jane said. "It's silly to waste the tickets."

"No, I'll stay with you."

"I don't want you to stay with me, Stedman."

"Well—"

"Go out with your law school friends. Talk about civil rights."

"Come on, Mary Jane. I'm not going to see them this trip."

"That's silly, Stedman. They're so charming and interesting—they've got *interesting* ideas."

"Well, they certainly are fond of you, Mary Jane," Stedman said, nodding. "In spite of what you think."

"Well, I'm not fond of them," Mary Jane said, stabbing her cigarette into the ash tray. "I'm sure not fond of them."

"Don't be difficult. I'm not going to see my friends, so there's no point even *talking*—"

"Oh, will you go see somebody? *Please!*" Mary Jane said. "I just can't *recuperate* with you hanging around." She took a deep breath. "And why don't you change your suit. It looks like you slept in it."

"Well, I did," he said.

"Oh, brilliant."

Stedman walked to the window. It had begun to rain, and the park was nearly deserted. The sky was dark gray. He had a slight headache, and he didn't know what to do; he didn't know what to say. He thought he'd let the tickets go, it was no tragedy. The other tickets he'd bought, he'd hold on to, for Mary Jane might be better tomorrow. He thought of going over to the theater district in an effort to exchange the tickets for that evening, or possibly get a refund, but it was too complicated and he'd just let them go, or possibly he'd just give them to somebody in the street, but it would be too embarrassing. Outside there was a traffic snarl on Fifty-ninth Street, with a lot of angry horn-blowing, and it seemed that everyone was carrying an umbrella. But in spite of everything—the rainy day, the confusion on the streets, it appeared to Stedman that all the people he could see were happy while he was miserable. He could take a walk, he thought, and get wet, or he could sit in the lobby and read the paper, or he could go into the coffee shop near the Plaza and read the paper there and then come back and sit in the lobby, and then he could possibly telephone some of his friends and have a chat. Then he could have another cup of coffee, or possibly go to the Guggenheim. Suddenly smiling, he turned around and looked at Mary Jane. "Look, I could get a deck of cards."

"Oh, please get out of here, Stedman. I'm tired. I don't feel well—please! Leave me alone."

He went into the bathroom and shaved and showered, and then he changed his suit. Before he left, he sat down on Mary Jane's bed. There was perspiration on her forehead and above her upper lip. He took out his handkerchief and tried to wipe it away, but she immediately jerked away from him and moved to the far side of the bed.

"Is there anything I can get for you?" he said.

She sighed and said nothing.

"Well, I'll see you later, sweetheart," he said.

When he had gone, Mary Jane got out of bed and put on her blue bathrobe, walked slowly into the bathroom and washed her face and brushed her teeth, and then she sat in front of her dressing-table mirror and combed and brushed her hair. She was feeling very weak, and she put down her hairbrush and placed her cheek on the tabletop; she felt herself falling asleep. She was so drowsy, and she forced herself to get up and get back into bed. She dozed off for an hour, and woke up hearing the wind and the rain against the windows. She was drenched with perspiration, and she was too tired to get up and take off her robe. "Oh, Mama," she said, weakly. "Where are you? How are you?" She drifted into a reverie, and thought of her childhood. Wiping her brow with the edge of her sheet, she remembered the pure time when everything was so sweet and loving and warm-hearted, and now she was sick in New York. She coughed. "Oh, Mama, how's Daddy and Raleigh, how's Carla and Chester?" she said, and then she began to cry. She quickly stopped, biting her lip, and then took a deep breath. "Oh, hell," she said, taking a Kleenex and blowing her nose. "I'm just so glad you got out of here, Stedman."

He had been so nice at first, she thought, but then he just *turned* on her. Well, he had turned on her family, and that was the same thing, and then it all started to break into pieces, and in all kinds of subtle ways Stedman began to act half crazy, and she got confused. He began to dwell on her family, how they *embarrassed* him.

"They're all pleasant and charming anachronisms," he told her after they'd been married a few months, and she had believed him, feeling hurt and afraid. Her own family had begun to embarrass her after only a few week ends of listening to Stedman's ideas. She remembered how her mother had embarrassed her down in Roanoke when she and Stedman had first begun to get serious. Her mother had pulled Stedman aside and recounted the family history and told him how her great-grandfather had ridden with J.E.B. Stuart. And Mary Jane had so wished that her mother would not refer to Negroes as *darkies* and Negro children as *pickaninnies,* and once when they were all sitting in the living room watching a television newscast which showed Negroes in a noisy demonstration over civil rights, her mother got extremely upset and said, "Oh, please turn it off. What are they doing? What do they think they're doing? And look at those white boys and girls in the demonstration, *too.* Look how they're agitating them up. It's disgraceful. Those Negroes show no *courtesy* or respect. Now how are they going to get their rights, if they're so disrespectful? If you ask for something, you should be *nice*—that's just common sense. Why, those ignorant darkies are just running around like *fools.* Did you ever see anything like it?" And Mary Jane had said, "But, Mama, they just want their rights," and her mother said, "Oh, Mary Jane, please, please!—and I'm sure Stedman agrees—that it's getting so you can't turn on the news without seeing Negroes doing something *unpleasant,* something disrespectful and *unrefined,* and let's have no more discussion about civil rights and *Negroes,*" and Mary Jane had said, "But Mama, they just want their rights, and you can't blame them for not being polite, and—"

"Oh, Mary Jane, please! I'm telling you, *please!*"

After they were married, Stedman never let her forget her background. "It's a dying society, Mary Jane. You're part of a dying society. Why do you think your mother's always talking about the past? Because there's no glory in her future—"

Mary Jane became furious when Stedman criticized

her family, even though she half believed him. "You don't understand them, Stedman. You have no sympathy. Now my mother is refined. You don't know anything about refinement, so you just can't understand what happens to a really refined personality when everything's changing, when everything she knew and thought was right and beautiful is just falling apart. You don't know a thing about refinement. You're all crudity. To you, crudity is a way of life. You think if you're real crude, it makes you seem honest. Oh, you're so misguided, Sted." And once they were sitting in the kitchen in Roanoke having coffee with her brother Raleigh, who was sixteen then. When Stedman asked him if he wanted the cream, Raleigh said, "No, sir. I like my coffee black and my women white," and Mary Jane was mortified, and she looked at Stedman, who smiled politely. Later, after they were married, Stedman often during coffee would bring up Raleigh's remark, and he would tell all of their friends about "Mary Jane's little brother, Raleigh, and his black coffee." It had caused her some pain and embarrassment, and she had always tried to defend her brother, at least in the beginning of their marriage, when she was still trying to talk to Stedman. "Sted, there's no kinder or gentler person than Raleigh, so why don't you stop going on about that stupid coffee joke. He didn't mean anything by it. He's just a kid. Sure he's a little backward and naïve about the race question, but he's fine and decent—just like my parents. Look, we hate rednecks and violence just as much as you. My family may be somewhat blind about their own feelings or responsibility, but, lord, Sted, they're nice people—much nicer than you, really. They're much kinder toward you than you are toward them. You're always making fun of them behind their backs, and they're always saying nice things about you behind yours. You just feel so superior, and I feel sorry for you. I really do. Look, my daddy saved a colored boy's life in the Second World War right near the Rhine River, and he got a Silver Star. Daddy would never even *talk* about it, he's just so damned modest—but he just did it naturally, just ran out and pulled that wounded colored boy in, and he risked his life. I read the citation, and you just sit around and make fun of him—"

"I was not attacking your father, Mary Jane," Stedman had said. "And besides, your *daddy's* Silver Star is irrelevant. You get everything all mixed up and tangled in your mind, and you miss the main point. I'm not attacking your goddam family—"

"Oh, you're such a liar, Stedman. You hate Southerners. You do. You're all full of hate, just like your poor old mother. Oh, yes you are. You hate anybody with a Southern accent. God knows why you married me . . ."

He could make her feel so bad sometimes. She thought about their conversation about Pullman porters. Oh what a mistake that was, she thought, to tell him how she loved Pullman porters. He just got it all wrong. She had said that she had always enjoyed long trips on the train because of the Negro Pullman porters, that they had a wonderful quality, and that it was a shame that it was all going to die out, and Stedman had said, "I know, Mary Jane, you'd like all Negroes to be like Pullman porters and go around bowing and scraping and treating you like the Queen of the Plantation."

"Oh, Stedman, you are so *unobservant*. Pullman porters have a great pride and dignity and independence, and they aren't at all *servile*—and they are fine men with great courtesy and *humor*."

And she got so angry when he went on about the white power structure, and how they had just denied the Negroes the opportunity to have decent jobs, so they had to spend their lives travelling on trains serving white men, without any chance of settling down and living normal lives.

"Oh, shut up, Stedman," she said. "Who's talking about that?"

Stedman made her conscious of the smallest, most trifling thing, she thought, like her brother's remark "I like my coffee black and my women white," which she had never paid the least attention to until she had met him. Stedman said it wasn't the remark *per se* but its *implications*. I'm just so tired of all his implications, she thought. She couldn't even say, "That's damn white of you," without Stedman getting upset. And there was the time she had laughed at an old Amos and Andy program on the radio, and he had given her a lecture on her condescension toward the Negro race, and about her desire to *perpetuate certain attitudes*.

"But it was funny, Stedman, damn you. It was *funny*. I've told you a hundred times I'm for civil rights, and I am. I know I've got a lot to learn, that I've got problems. I admit it. I don't think all Negroes are like they are on Amos and Andy. But the characters on Amos and Andy are *funny*, Stedman, damn you."

And she smiled when she remembered how Stedman's reactions had been so predictable. She could practically make him salivate like Pavlov's dog, like the time they were watching an old haunted house movie on television at three in the morning, and there was a scene in which an old Negro had just seen a ghost. He got scared, rolled his eyes, and then passed out. She laughed mainly to get under Stedman's skin, and then she had partly lied, in saying, "You're so pompous, so unnatural, Stedman. It was *very, very* funny." Then she gave an imitation of the Negro's rolling his eyes and passing out. Stedman gave her a long lecture about "stereotypes" and "propaganda against the Negro race."

She recalled the time Stedman took her to witness the civil rights march and demonstration in Washington. She remembered that he wouldn't let her just watch it and hear the speeches, but he was *explaining* everything, and she told him to please be quiet for a while, that she wasn't stupid and was capable of understanding things for herself, and to please shut up for a while. "Oh, Stedman, they all came down on these buses from New York," she had said, looking at him to get its effect. "The girls are so frumpy, look at their clothes, all dressed alike in jeans and baggy sweaters and carrying signs. They're a sight, Stedman. Oh, I know they mean well. No doubt they do." Watching the demonstration outside the White House, she had thought of her mother, imagined the look of confusion on her face, as she watched the white men with beards, and colored girls and colored boys, and white girls, this rhythmically marching picket line of happy, singing, clapping people. And, oh, they were funny, she thought. It was *amusing*. There was this tall Negro boy—he must have been seven feet tall, Mary Jane thought, like some Watusi, and he was leading the freedom chant, holding a sign, bending and swaying to the clapping, "Free ee dom, Free ee dom, Free ee dom, Freed*om,* Freed*om*—Ohh, Free ee dom, Free ee dom, Free ee dom, Freed*om,* Freed*om.*" She and Stedman were standing behind two white policemen, and one said to the other, "That's the Kawabuki tribe. They're getting ready for a lion hunt," and Mary Jane had started to laugh, and Stedman, in a paroxysm of shame, grabbed her roughly and pulled her away, telling her that she was an awful little fascist, just like the cops. Half the time she hardly knew what she felt, whether she was reacting to what she saw or whether she was responding to Stedman's bossy, intimidating moral lectures and his constant criticism. He went on about the demonstrators, she remembered. "You make fun of these people, Mary Jane, and you don't just realize the depth and strength of their commitment—so many of them are sincere and have sacrificed a great deal for their beliefs and suffered hardship—and often at great inconvenience to themselves and sometimes at great risk—and you make fun of them. It wouldn't hurt you to have a little more commitment yourself, Mary Jane—"

"Oh, who cares? I don't like them," she yelled at him. "They're so damned smug, just like you, Stedman—and they have this awful fanatical look in their eye, and most of them are so *righteous* and full of *hatred*—and they're just a bunch of show-offs. I'd be damned if I'd ever join hands with them and sing 'We Shall Overcome.' It would just stick in my throat. Why didn't you marry a freedom rider, Stedman—instead of a Southern girl? You just make me tired . . ."

"Mary Jane, you're a moral mess. You really are," he had said.

"Oh, shut up. *Please!*"

Shaking his head, Stedman had said, "You'll never change. You're all alike—your father and mother and your little brother, Raleigh . . ."

"Oh, damn you, Stedman," she had screamed at him. "Don't you ever criticize my family again. Don't you dare. My family is *kind* to Negroes. We like Negroes better and more completely and more honestly than you could ever understand. Do you hear me, Stedman? It's not our fault we don't have your brilliant liberal experience. But we have always loved and been nice to our colored people—and we have been loved in return—oh, lord, our cook, Carla, she's been with us for fifty years. She raised me—she raised Raleigh, and she raised my mother and *her* brother, my uncle Dan. And Carla's son, Chester, grew up with me and Raleigh, and Raleigh loves him like a brother, and my daddy's putting Chester through *college*, damn you, and Chester's just a fine young man. And Daddy said he couldn't like him more if he was his own *son*. Why, Chester and Raleigh went hunting together as boys with rifles my daddy *gave* them for Christmas, just out in the fields all day with a lunch that Carla had made for them, and hunting together until the sun went down . . ."

Stedman had contorted his face.

"You don't understand a goddam thing! It's all so crazy. Just tell me this. Did Chester ever have dinner at your table?"

"No! Because Carla'd be embarrassed. Don't you understand? Why are you so insensitive? It just wouldn't be right, Stedman. Chester'd just feel awkward with Carla *serving*. But Daddy's just paying his way through agricultural college and has spoken to him many times in his study, talking man to man, and Chester loves him, damn you!"

Stedman laughed.

"Look, it's all so damn paternalistic, and you know it . . ."

"Paternalistic. *Paternalistic,*" Mary Jane mimicked. "Oh, lord, you're rich, Stedman. I just told you that Daddy treats him like a son, so I guess it is paternalistic, Stedman, I mean talk to me, and don't parrot your lawyer friends. That's all I ask of you . . ."

He shook his head, took off his glasses, and sighed.

"You're a moral mess, Mary Jane. I feel sorry for you."

"You know Stedman, the thing is, we have *sympathy.* We really do. I mean with all our problems about the race question, we still have that. But you just have a guilty conscience, and you make everybody miserable, particularly yourself. Oh, Stedman, you just feel so guilty about Negroes—about everything—and you feel so guilty all the time. Oh, I feel sorry for you, Stedman, I really do."

I'm just tired of it all, she thought, lying on her bed at the Plaza. If we could have only had a child, I would have been happy as sin, and Stedman could have gone on about his political action and left me in peace, and I'd have had something else to think about. It was so ridiculous, she thought. They had all these problems in their marriage, and all they ever seemed to talk about was Negroes. But they had even stopped talking about Negroes lately. She didn't think Stedman would ever talk about Negroes again, and she knew why, and she even felt truly sorry for him, in spite of everything.

* * *

MARY JANE took her temperature. It was ninety-nine degrees F. Her sore throat was not as painful. The cold was rising into her head. She took a Kleenex tissue from the box on the night table and blew her nose and wiped her eyes. Her eyes were burning and she had a headache. Oh, lord, she thought, I'm getting so hateful and mean. She wondered what Stedman was doing, and then, gradually, looking serene and sad, she drifted off to sleep.

After reading the paper and having coffee, Stedman had called some friends, but they were out to lunch. He sat in the lobby for a while, afraid to return to the room and disturb Mary Jane, and then went out and walked in the rain. It was raining lightly when he started out, but after he had gone a few blocks from the hotel, the rain began to come down harder. The wind whipped it in his face, and Stedman found it very refreshing. It was healthy, he thought, and good for his complexion. He felt very relaxed. He thought of how Mary Jane always told him to relax, and half the time he never knew what she meant, and that if she had been with him then and he had said to her, "I feel relaxed, Mary Jane, walking in the rain. Is this what you mean?" and he knew she would have said, "No, that's not what I mean, Stedman. That's not what I mean at all."

Stedman walked along. Gradually, the refreshment turned to discomfort. The rain soaked through his coat and shoes and went down his neck. By the time he reached First Avenue, he was cold and depressed. He stopped in a small bar and ordered a double Scotch and drank it slowly. Feeling warmer, he had another with a glass of water as a chaser. Standing at the bar, he conceived the idea of buying a bottle of Scotch and taking it back to the hotel. They would just sit around and have a few drinks, making their own little Palm Court in the room. The trip didn't have to be a complete disaster, he thought, and perhaps a few drinks might provide the atmosphere for reconciliation. The idea filled him with hope. When he reached the street again, he hardly noticed the rain, and he walked twenty more blocks, just for the joy of it, before stopping at a liquor store and purchasing a fifth of Johnny Walker Black Label. Then he walked aimlessly for about an hour and a half, finally hailing a cab back to the hotel. It was about three in the afternoon, still gray clouds and rain, when he returned to their room.

Mary Jane was asleep. Stedman took off his wet clothes and shoes and socks. He laid his suit and overcoat on the floor, then went into the bathroom, bringing out a towel and two glasses, and sat down in a soft chair near a small table by the window. He put the glasses, along with the bottle of Johnny Walker, on the table, poured two drinks, and then proceeded to dry his feet with the towel. He was feeling very good, refreshed, confident, and relaxed.

When Mary Jane woke up, she saw Stedman sitting across the room, smiling in his underwear, a towel over his feet, his hand on a table with a bottle of whiskey and two glasses, each a third full. Behind him was the window, and outside the rain and the wind. She sat up in her blue bathrobe and rubbed her eyes, then looked at Stedman with irritation.

Still smiling, Stedman said, "How are you feeling, Mary Jane?"

"What are you doing, Stedman? What do you think you're doing?" she said.

"I'm having a drink. And I thought we'd have one together."

"What are you trying to *do,* Stedman?"

"I'm trying to talk to you," Stedman said, suddenly looking fatuous and belligerent. "Damn it, don't give me your hunt club look."

"My what?" she said.

"You heard me."

She sighed.

"You know, Stedman, I can't stand deprived people."

"Who's deprived?" Stedman said, picking up a glass of Scotch and sipping it.

"You are, Stedman. Emotionally deprived and ungenerous and gross and self-righteous. You're *deprived.*" She began to cough and her face got red.

He put down the glass and swallowed. She had managed to hurt his feelings again. He took a deep breath, looked down at his feet and blushed, then picked up the two glasses and walked over to the bed.

"I don't want a drink!" she said, pressing her back against the headboard of the bed.

Stedman laughed.

"What's the matter with you? Come on, it can't hurt you, and I'll sit in the chair," he said.

He put the glass on the night table by her bed and then went back to the chair and sat down.

"You keep away," she said.

"I'm not going to touch you."

She suddenly laughed, then tears appeared, and she pulled a Kleenex from the box and wiped her eyes.

Stedman came over and put his arms around her. She pushed him away. "Now just go away," she said quietly. "Go away now."

He went back to the chair and sat down. Mary Jane swallowed some Scotch and lit a cigarette. Her long hair was partly over one eye and spread out over the right shoulder of her bathrobe. Stedman thought she looked beautiful. The drink and the coughing had added color to her face, and she had that highly nervous, sensitive edge which frightened Stedman but made her appear lovely.

Mary Jane coughed and blew her nose, then put out her cigarette and folded her arms across her chest. She felt very fluttery, particularly her hands, and by folding her arms and pressing, she felt she could contain herself. She wished Stedman would go away and not just sit there gaping at her. He poured himself another drink, then came over with the bottle and poured some Scotch in her glass. He went back to the chair and sat down again.

"Well, what would you like to do?" Stedman said, smiling. "I could turn on the television."

"What do you want from me, Stedman?"

"Let's talk," he said, looking very solemn. "Really."

"O.K., let's talk," she said, picking up her glass and swallowing some Scotch. She put the glass down and laughed. "Let's sing 'We Shall Overcome.' "

"Let's not start all that," Stedman said, looking very serious.

"Oh, let's *do,* Stedman," she said, beginning to hum "We Shall Overcome," then took a sip of Scotch and lit a cigarette.

"You shouldn't smoke if you're sick," he said.

"How do the words go? 'Black and white together or something . . . We shall overcome, etcetera.' "

"Please, Mary Jane," Stedman said, shaking his head. "You're not feeling well. Let's not get into any acrimonious—"

"You wanted to talk. Let's talk about Brandon," Mary Jane said, sitting up, her eyes flashing.

Stedman reddened.

"Look, I don't want to talk about him."

"You're a coward, Stedman. You really are."

There was a slight tremor of his lower lip. He stood up, then walked into the bathroom and closed the door and turned on the cold-water tap, letting it run. He heard her yell, "Tell me about your social conscience, Stedman." He remained in the bathroom, staring at the sink and trying to get control of himself. She always ended up putting him in the wrong, he thought. He bent over and put his head under the cold-water tap.

Mary Jane closed her eyes and thought of the party Stedman had taken her to in Washington, about six months before, in a small house in Georgetown. There Stedman had wanted to introduce her to four or five Negroes who were active in certain civil rights groups. They were down from New York. It was part of Stedman's educational program to introduce her to Negroes in a social situation, and this was her first real social experience. Stedman had told her that she should try to see them as independent human beings and not merely as members of a servant class as she had known them all her life. ("But I've always seen them as individual and independent human beings, Stedman," she had said to him.) Many of Stedman's white lawyer friends and their wives had also been at the party, and they had behaved, in Mary Jane's view, in a very obnoxious, artificial way. They had tried so hard, she thought, to be emancipated and enlightened, and it had saddened and depressed her. She felt that it wasn't the Negroes being there that had bothered her, it wasn't her background getting in the way, at least not altogether—it was just that they all lacked honesty, as though they were just *pretending* in that company that certain problems didn't really exist. It was a strain. But worst of all, she felt they were all too smug, felt too good about themselves and their personal moral position in the world, lacking any kind of true, natural humility and sensitivity. Feeling a little uncertain at first about how she could get into a pleasant conversation with the Negroes, she had talked instead to some of the wives, and then, after they had been at the party for an hour, as she was about to get up her courage and make an approach, a Negro named Brandon, slightly built and middle-aged, with what she remembered as "this awfully affected little beard" and finely cut suit, had become, in her view, insultingly familiar with her, and she had just wanted to scream. He had put his hand on her arm and said, "I hear you're from down near Roanoke. So am I. Funny I never knew you," he said, looking around at Stedman, who had just come over, wearing what Mary Jane remembered as a "sickening, artificial smile."

"Yes, it's kind of strange," she said, looking at Stedman.

"Well, baby, it's strange all right, but I won't hold it

against you," Brandon said, putting his arm around her waist. "Say, let's dance."

"I don't hear any music," Mary Jane said, feeling mortified, thinking, Oh, lord, poor Daddy would just die. Poor Raleigh. Poor Mama. And then she was slightly ashamed of herself for thinking that.

"We'll make our own music," Brandon said, holding tight to her arm. "Let's sing 'Dixie.' "

She flushed, yanked her arm free, and yelled,

"Oh, you just get away from me. You hear?" and she walked away from him, into the bedroom, and got her coat. Brandon started singing, "Oh, I wish I was in the land of cotton, old times there are not forgotten . . ."

Stedman took her home.

She had cried and screamed at him.

"You were just too stupid or cowardly to see it. He just started on me because I'm Southern, and he just wanted to show everybody how he could embarrass me. He was trying to *hurt* me. He put his hands on me. He knew I wasn't used to a colored man doing that. I know I've got problems, but I wanted to be nice to him, and he was just so intent on *humiliating* me. But you all were just so *emancipated,* and this Brandon was such a *hero* because he's black and can humiliate a Southern girl, and you're such an awful, gross coward, Stedman. You really are. You should have seen the forced, unnatural, cowardly smile on your face, and I swear you just can't see—or you're unwilling to see—what a miserable nothing that Brandon is, just so cruel and untender and mean and vindictive, with his awful little beard and his pathological desire for *revenge.* He's really sick, that boy, and you let him embarrass and torment me, because you were afraid, Stedman, afraid they'd kick you out of the liberal union. You were too much of a coward to stand up for your own wife, and you let that uppity Brandon *humiliate* me. I know I've got problems. But what about you? You and all your sheeplike lawyer friends with their awful, dowdy, uncharming wives, and yes, Stedman, you all think you're so anti-racist, part of the new order, so damn superior—oh, why don't you please look inside yourself and see what a pathetic disgusting mess you are. God, how I hate you, Stedman. You lack character. You really do."

She was sorry she had used the word "uppity" to describe Brandon; she didn't mean it the way it sounded. Stedman, later on that same night, had accused her of referring to Brandon as that "uppity coon," and she began to cry. "Oh, you're such a liar, Stedman. You're such a liar. I know I've got problems, but I never said that, and I've got problems, God knows, but so have you. Oh my, your case history would be interesting, Stedman, a hundred years from now."

STEDMAN STOOD in the bathroom, his hands on the sink, leaning forward and breathing heavily. Everything was falling apart; he could just feel it falling into little pieces. He took a towel and dried his hair. Christ, he thought, I wish there were another way out of the bathroom. He couldn't face her. She could make him so damned afraid, and she'd probably bring up the *other* thing. She could be a real horror, he thought. He suddenly thought of his mother. She appeared to him sitting in his father's study, surrounded by journals and periodicals, with an intense look of long-suffering on her face, reading. He put his head under the faucet again, then wrapped the towel around his head. He decided he would leave the bathroom very calm, as though nothing had happened, and no matter what Mary Jane said to him, he would ignore her. He would put on his clothes and take another walk until he was all right again.

When Stedman walked out of the bathroom, Mary Jane was standing by the chair, pouring herself another drink. She drank it down and made a face.

"Damn, Stedman, why don't you put your pants on or something!" she said, walking across the room and getting into bed. "You look so gross. You know you're just going to fat, and you're looking so *old.*"

Stedman reddened, walked over to the table, and poured himself a drink, then picked up his wet pants from the floor and put them on. He sat down in the chair, feeling cold and clammy around his legs, and then drank the Scotch. He said nothing. Pursing his lips, he began to breathe consciously, deeply and slowly.

"Let's talk, Stedman," she said, smiling maliciously. He shook his head.

"Oh, I see. You just want to sit there and fill yourself up with air, like the Goodyear blimp—"

"Please, I—"

"You *what!*"

"Nothing."

Stedman put his head in his hands. He was suddenly too tired to put his clothes on; he wanted to take off his wet pants, but he was afraid of provoking her. He wondered how long he could leave his hands over his face without her saying anything. I'll just count to ten, he thought, and then move my hands away, a very smooth and natural transition, and then I'll yawn and fall asleep in the chair. His head ached and felt heavy. He forgot to count, letting his hands fall limply on his lap. He kept his eyes closed.

"Stedman!"

He opened his eyes.

"Tell me about your social conscience," she said.

He shook his head.

Mary Jane licked her lips; she was breathing rapidly and her face was flushed. A small vein on her forehead had slightly protruded and was throbbing. Drops of perspiration were on her temples. She began to cough, turning redder. She held up a hand, as if to say, "Don't go away. I'm not through with you."

"Stedman," she said, wiping her eyes. "Do you *really* care about Emerging Africa?"

He took a deep breath and looked pained. Then he poured some more Scotch in his glass.

"That's it. Drink yourself to death," she said. "Crawl into your private world where you're just so fine and *humane* and *not* selfish and cowardly and blind—and *sick.*"

"Shut your goddam mouth!" Stedman yelled.

She shook her head and sighed.

"O.K., Stedman, I wasn't going to do this. I promised myself I'd never hit a person when he's so *obviously* down, but you're such a nasty, foul bastard. What about the Fraziers?"

He stiffened, looking trapped.

"Oh, I don't remember—"

"Shut up, you coward."

"Don't tell me to shut up," Stedman said, standing up.

"I'm telling you to shut up. Shut up. So you've forgotten the Fraziers. That's *convenient.* You never let me forget anything. Well, I'm sure as hell not letting you forget the Fraziers."

Stedman sat down, then picked up his glass and emptied it, then closed his eyes and bit his lower lip.

Mary Jane brushed her hair back from her eyes and smiled.

The Fraziers were a couple they'd had lunch with in Washington three weeks before. Frazier, a Negro, was a lawyer who had come down from New York to talk to Stedman about the implications of certain legislative hearings. He had brought his wife down with him, and Stedman had suggested that Frazier and his wife have lunch with Mary Jane and him. He thought it would be good for her, one more corrective experience. Mary Jane had been agreeable, and, after meeting at Stedman's office, they had all gone out to lunch together. She had liked the Fraziers right from the start, found them attractive and charming, particularly the girl, Sylvia, who was very warm and kind. She had enjoyed herself, and it was pleasant and natural—all except for Stedman, who she thought kept looking at her, as though he were judging her performance. She had ignored him, and just talked to the Fraziers. She really did enjoy them. It had occurred to her what her parents might think—and her brother Raleigh, and even Carla—what they would think of her having lunch with a Negro man and woman just as though there was no real difference, but she'd found it no real effort at all. She just liked them and hardly thought about their being Negroes. They were nothing like Brandon. But halfway through the meal she'd noticed Stedman in some distress. He'd been relatively quiet and incommunicative during lunch, and toward the end of the meal, smiling with embarrassment, he seemed ill and pleaded that he wasn't feeling well. After saying goodbye to the Fraziers, he did not go back to his office, but went home for the rest of the day. Mary Jane kept asking him what was the matter, for aside from appearing physically ill, he seemed demoralized and ashamed. Later that night, after they'd made love, when he was open and trusting and vulnerable, and desperate to confess, he told her why he had become ill: he "sometimes" couldn't eat with Negroes; he didn't know why, but it made him sick. He had tried to fight it and understand it, but it had remained a desperate problem. When he ate with Negroes, he became nauseated. It was something about watching them eat their food. It was the same in the Army. He thought he had gotten over it, but he was sadly mistaken. She had comforted him, told him not to worry, that he would get better; and he had never been more grateful for consolation in his whole life.

"SO YOU REALLY just went and forgot, Stedman," Mary Jane said, clutching the collar of her robe. "Well, well, that's nice. Of all the damned hypocrites—all your talk about brotherly love and equal rights and justice and helping the Negro, and it turns out you can't even eat with one without hardly puking at the table. That's just fine, Stedman. I ate with Negroes all my life—with Carla and my nurses—and it wasn't any different for me than eating with my brother or my parents—but you're such a morally superior person from Buffalo, New York, and you've got to *puke* if a Negro sits down at the same table—"

"Shut up!" Stedman screamed. He got up from the chair and kicked out at the table. The lamp went crashing to the floor; the base broke in half. "You Southern bitch!" Stedman screamed, going over to her bed. He lunged for her and grabbed her by the shoulders and began to shake her. She screamed up at him. "You Yankee bastard! You carpetbagging Yankee bastard!" She swung her arms against his chest; her hair fell over her eyes. Stedman ripped her bathrobe at the shoulders, and then he hit her in the face with an open hand. Her lip began to bleed. She screamed, then leaped out of the bed at him. Stedman grabbed her by the arms and threw her violently against the headboard of the bed. She tried to get up and fell on the floor, and then, moaning and crying, she got to her feet again and came at him, screaming. "You son of a bitch bastard. You better kill me—" She swung and hit him in the face, knocking his glasses off. Stedman, his wet pants clinging to his legs, his undershirt ripped, stooped over to pick up his glasses, suddenly realizing what he had done. She was pounding him on the back. He straightened up and tried to avoid her. "Oh, my God," he yelled. "Please, Mary Jane." She swung at him one more time, missed, and fell, exhausted and coughing, onto the bed, and then she began to sob.

Breathing with difficulty, Stedman went into the bathroom and soaked a washcloth in cold water, squeezed it out, then returned to the room and sat down on the bed with Mary Jane. He wiped her forehead and dabbed her bleeding lip. "God, I'm so sorry, I'm so terribly sorry—" he kept saying. He wiped her tears. She lay on her back. Gradually her breathing became regular, and she stopped crying. She looked at him without anger, feeling a great relief. Taking Stedman's hand, she said, "Sted, I want a divorce. Please don't say anything now. I've been thinking about it for a long time."

He tried to say something, but she raised a hand over his mouth and shook her head. "Please, Sted, I won't change my mind," she said weakly, and then she closed her eyes and fell off to sleep.

Stedman returned to the bathroom, taking off his glasses and wiping his face with the washcloth. His mouth was open, though he had ceased to breathe rapidly. He looked at himself in the mirror and hardly recognized his reflection, which seemed monstrous and deformed. Sitting on the edge of the bathtub, he became briefly overwhelmed with terror and guilt; then it passed, and he felt nothing but exhaustion. Washing his face and his hands, he returned to the bedroom, took off his pants, and got into bed.

Neither Mary Jane nor Stedman had dinner but slept through until morning.

SUNLIGHT CAME IN through the window. Stedman awoke feeling sick with guilt. Mary Jane was coughing. She was dressed in a blue skirt and red sweater and was placing her suitcase on the baggage stand at the foot of the bed. Her lip was slightly swollen with a small scab at the corner of her mouth. It amazed him how beautiful she looked, how serene and lovely and clear-eyed. The bottle of Johnny Walker was still on the floor, along with the broken lamp.

"How are you feeling, Mary Jane?"

"I've just got a slight cold now, Stedman. I'm all right," she said.

"Why are you packing?" he said.

She took a deep breath, sighed and walked over to the night table and lit a cigarette. "Look, Sted, what I said last night, I meant—oh, let's not talk about it now. I'm too tired. I'm too tired of talking."

She walked into the bathroom and closed the door.

Mary Jane had breakfast alone at a coffee shop near the hotel. Stedman remained in the room and ordered his breakfast from room service. The sunlight was so strong and the air was so clear that he found it hard to believe that she was really leaving him. Holding a piece of toast, he walked over to the window and looked out at the park. The skaters were going around the rink in their blue and yellow coats. He could see them so clearly, and he thought he could hear music.

After packing his bag, Stedman called the garage and requested his car. Twenty minutes later, the garage called to tell him that there was something wrong with the fuel line or carburetor, and that, with his authorization, a mechanic would be sent for. Sitting down at the desk, Stedman wrote a short note to Mary Jane, telling her of the delay. Then he left for the garage to oversee the repairs.

They left New York at five-thirty that afternoon. They hardly said a word all the way down the New Jersey Turnpike. Stedman was afraid to talk. Mary Jane had no desire to.

She crouched forward and tried to sleep with her head on top of the padded dashboard, but later placed her arms and head against the window frame of the door.

After they'd crossed the Susquehanna River, about

ten miles south, they got a flat tire, and without saying a word, with a barely audible groan, Stedman pulled over to the shoulder of the road, got out of the car, and went into the trunk for the spare tire, the jack, and the tire iron; and then he opened the door on Mary Jane's side, and looking briefly at her, his eyes full of apology, he went into the glove compartment for the flashlight. "You better stay in and keep warm," he said.

It was so quiet and wonderful, Mary Jane thought, without the hum of the engine, without moving so fast through the countryside, and she got out of the car, her arms folded against her camel's-hair coat. Oh, everything's just so pure here, she thought, looking up at the fleecy clouds and the three-quarter moon, and then at Stedman who seemed then so kind and innocent and vulnerable, with that quality of sweetness he had when she married him. He was trying to put the jack lift under the frame and hold the flashlight at the same time, pressed against his rib cage by his upper arm. Mary Jane thought his face seemed so hurt in the reflected light, and he seemed half blind, even with his glasses. It was so wonderful, she thought, the feeling she felt then. She wished she could spend the rest of her life, even all eternity, having this feeling, just loving Stedman, watching him change the tire, looking up at the sky of pale winter stars near the Susquehanna, not thinking or caring about ugly social change and all the rest of it. She felt she really loved him then, that she loved everyone. Her cold was breaking up. She could breathe freely and felt slightly intoxicated by the cold, clear air; suddenly, she had a brief, tender feeling for Stedman's mother, who flashed into her mind, and for awful Brandon with his awful beard and ignorant ways, and for the whole miserable world. Stedman picked up the spare tire and dropped it, then picked it up again, accidentally kicking the flashlight. Tears welled up in Mary Jane's eyes. He's so confused, she thought, and I'm so confused, and now we're just going to have to part forever. She knew they could never really reconcile in a deep way, and though it truly grieved her to leave him, she was already in her mind's eye taking her pictures off the wall and packing her bags, and going home to Daddy.

Jack Kelsey's All-Stars, 1941

SEPTEMBER 1941.

I just finished playing with Jack Kelsey's All-Stars. Before I went up to Baltimore and tried out, I played ball in a fast industrial league in North Carolina. I played second base and did just fine. I'm from near High Point, and I'll be fifteen next May.

Jack Kelsey met my train in Baltimore on a Saturday night. He was a big man, all right, about six feet four and two hundred and fifty. He was close to sixty-five years old. He was smoking a big cigar, and he was real well dressed in this brown summer suit and a panama straw hat and brown-and-white shoes. I was all dressed up myself.

"So you're Billy John Lansdowne," Jack said, looking me over.

"Yes, sir," I said.

We shook hands.

"You sure look small for fourteen," he said.

That was pretty good. I'm five feet eight and one hundred and forty.

"Well, come on, Billy," he said, and he picked up my suitcase and carried it out to his car.

He drove me over to the Lord Baltimore Hotel in this big Buick. We didn't say too much. He showed me how to register for my room, but I signed in myself.

"So you play second base," Jack said as we went up on the elevator. He carried my suitcase and a cardboard box he had taken from the back seat of his car.

He showed me the room, opening drawers and closet doors and turning on all the lights. He asked me to look at the view out the window, but I couldn't see too much.

It was really a nice room. I sat down on a desk chair and watched Jack walk around and puff on his cigar. Then he threw the cardboard box on the bed and told me to open it. There was a baseball uniform inside.

"Try it on," Jack said.

I took off my clothes and got into the uniform. On the front of the shirt was KELSEY'S ALL-STARS. It was a little big for me.

"I'll have it cut down," Jack said. "If things work out."

We sat around in the hotel room for a while, and Jack kept asking me what was the matter. I said nothing was the matter.

"Are you sad?" Jack said.

"No, sir."

"Well, how do you like Baltimore?"

"I ain't seen it, Mr. Kelsey," I said, and Jack really started to laugh. He slapped me on the shoulder.

"Billy, maybe we'll get along," he said.

Jack asked me about the different teams I'd played for. He wanted to know how much experience I'd had and if I was really hitting .400 in the Three-City Tobacco and Furniture League.

"Well, tomorrow you're playing in a game," Jack said, blowing out some smoke. I said I didn't think the trip started until Tuesday, and Jack said that was true but there was a game down at Upper Marlboro in the morning. A lot of boys on his club were playing in it.

"They'll be playing for both teams," Jack said.

"Will Breen be there?" I said. Breen was a friend of mine from High Point. He played third base for Jack.

"No. He said he'd see you Monday," Jack said.

I wondered why Breen hadn't come and met the train like he'd promised. He was probably out horsing around.

"I'll get you in the game," Jack said, real serious. "I got to see how you play against men."

I didn't say anything. Jack asked me if I was sure I'd played against men players, and I said I was.

"Well, that's fine, Billy," he said. "Because I ain't looking for no mascot."

He got to his feet and put on his hat, and we shook hands again.

"I sure hope you make it," he said.

I walked him to the door, and Jack told me to go right to bed and not to listen to the radio. He said he'd call for me at nine in the morning.

"If you want something," Jack said, pointing at the phone, "just ask for room service."

But there was nothing I wanted, and I went right to sleep. I've never been so down in my life as that first night in Baltimore.

MY FATHER began to teach me how to play ball when I was two. When I was ten, I played in a fifteen-and-under league, and as I got older I moved higher up in the amateurs.

Some men from Carolina had told Jack about me, and he wrote to my daddy, inviting me to try out for the All-Stars. It was a barnstorming team he'd formed for the last five years, since 1936, to tour different northern towns. Most of the players were semipro, and three or four had played in the minors. They came from Virginia and Maryland. Every year Jack invited up a few young players from North Carolina. It was sort of a tradition, and it was an honor to be invited. I wasn't invited the first time around. It was Luther Breen and Frankie Wood that Jack invited first. Wood was Breen's age, seventeen. But after he came up to Baltimore, he got sick and had to have his appendix out, and he couldn't make the trip. That's when Jack invited me.

When it was time to go, my mother packed my suitcase and gave me five dollars for the train.

"Billy John," she said, "you want to go way up there?"

She acted like I was going off to prison and she'd never see me again, but I told her, "Don't worry, Mama. I'll be back in time for school."

WHEN JACK AND I started off for Marlboro, it was a fine, sunny morning. The sky was dark blue.

Jack had these field glasses around his neck. He puffed on his cigar and tapped the ashes out the car window.

We had breakfast on the road, in a little diner that looked like a railroad car. Jack ordered six eggs and a ham steak. Then he put a hand on top of my head and said, "Give my father anything he wants."

I had two fried eggs with sausage and pie and coffee. The waitress brought us about ten slices of toast. She really enjoyed watching us eat. She stood there with her arms folded, shaking her head.

"When did you all eat last?" she said.

Jack said we'd already had breakfast in Baltimore, but we needed a little snack to tide us over to lunch.

I was sitting there in my uniform, and the waitress said, "Who is Kelsey's All-Stars?" Jack said we were a Japanese softball team, and then he started laughing. When the waitress came back with some more toast, Jack told her that we were really a circus act. She laughed and said that we must have an eating act, and Jack said real serious that I walked the high wire, and when she asked him what he did, Jack said, "I catch him when he falls." After he nearly fell out of his chair laughing, he asked me to give her my autograph.

When we were through eating, he lit up a cigar and said, "Billy, how about another piece of pie?" But I was all filled up and just had another cup of coffee.

After we were on the road again, Jack began to sing this song called "Smiles." "There are smiles that make you happy, there are smiles that make you glad." That's all I remember. He sang it over and over while I looked out the window through his field glasses.

"Well, are you ready to play?" Jack said, later.

I nodded.

He told me about some of the players that were going to be at Marlboro that morning. About eleven of them would be playing for him. Jack said that the best players were Duke St. John and Fred Moore. They used to play in the Southern Association. Moore was over forty and

Duke was thirty-five. Most of the boys were in their middle and late twenties.

While I was looking out the window, Jack tapped me on the shoulder and said, "Billy, this game's for money. They ain't playing for fun." I was really surprised. Each player had to put up twenty dollars, like an ante; and there were side bets, too. "I'll put up your end," Jack said. "Twenty dollars?" I said, and Jack laughed. We didn't say anything for a while. I took some deep breaths. I'd never played in a game where there was betting on it, and Jack told me not to worry about the money. "Just play your normal game," he said, and I really began to get keyed up.

As we drove up to this little rickety ball park, Jack said, "O.K., put your spikes on. I'll meet you on the field."

While I sat on the fender of the car and laced up my spikes, Jack walked onto the field. All the players were really glad to see him.

"How you doing, Jack?" this big, red-faced boy said. He had MILLER PONTIAC across his shirt.

Jack was smiling wide, and he walked around and greeted everybody.

When I walked over to Jack, he was talking to this very tall man with a long face who had CHATTANOOGA across his shirt. He was at least six feet five, and he had a real wide mouth.

"Billy, this here is Fred Moore," Jack said.

We shook hands.

Moore ran one of the teams that was playing that morning. Jack had a talk with him about putting me in the game, but Moore said he had a set line-up.

"Well, you just change it," Jack said, real serious.

Moore smiled and slapped Jack on the shoulder.

"I can't change nothing, Jack," he said. "This game's for money."

Jack bit down on his cigar.

"You play him. Hear?"

"I can't play no kid," Moore said.

Jack got angry; he said I was a famous player from High Point and so forth. But it didn't make any impression on Fred Moore. It made even less on Duke St. John who ran the other team.

We went over to the third-base side and sat down on a bench halfway down the left-field line. Jack was burning up. He didn't like driving all the way down from Baltimore for nothing. I looked over at him, and I said, "Don't worry, Mr. Kelsey. It don't matter."

"It matters to me," Jack said. "Them bastards are going to play you yet."

We watched the game. I was glad I wasn't playing. I kept taking deep breaths and letting the air out slowly.

About the fifth inning, Jack got up and stretched and took off his coat and tie. "Billy, let's loosen up some," he said. He borrowed a ball and glove, and we warmed up real easy. "I guess they ain't going to play me, Mr. Kelsey," I said. After throwing about ten minutes, we sat down and watched the game again. There was no score, but in the seventh inning Moore hit a home run, and it was 1–0. And then in the top of the ninth, Bobby Cantrell, a player for Moore, hurt himself sliding into second base. They had to carry him off the field.

"Don't move," Jack said, getting up from the bench.

He walked over to Moore, and they began to talk.

Jack kept pointing at me, and Moore kept shaking his head. Then Jack got mad and pounded his fist into his hand. Finally, Moore just shrugged.

Jack walked back over to where I was sitting.

"How are you feeling?" he said.

"Fine."

"Well, you're going in at third for Moore's team."

He slapped me on the shoulder. I sure didn't feel like playing.

When I walked onto the field, not one of those boys said a word to me. The first baseman wouldn't even throw me a ground ball while the pitcher was warming up. He just threw to the other boys and left me out. Jack noticed and yelled something, but I still didn't get a throw. I felt strange. I wasn't used to playing third.

We were winning 1–0, and we just had to hold them in the ninth.

But after getting the first hitter to pop up to short, our pitcher, Joe Weber, walked the next two boys, and then he got the next hitter to tap right back to him. He threw to me for the force play. I took the throw and kicked out at third base without looking at it. I didn't feel anything. I'd missed the bag. By the time I found it, the runner was in safe at third, and the bases were loaded.

Fred Moore called time out. He walked over from short and Joe Weber came off the mound. Maynard Holmes, this big red-faced catcher, kicked his mask to the backstop, and he came walking out.

"What the hell is wrong with you!" Moore said. Then Holmes grabbed me and started to shake me, and I thought he was going to break my ribs. Jack came over there fast.

"Take your goddam hands off him!" Jack said, and he pushed Holmes away. Holmes kept saying I'd cost him fifty dollars.

"Why'd you bring him, Jack?" Moore kept saying.

Joe Weber acted like he would have killed me if he could have got away with it.

Jack told them all to shut up. The umpires told us to start the game right then or they were leaving, and we got ready to play.

The bases were loaded with one out. I took a quick look over at Jack sitting on the bench. He was leaning forward with his head in his hands. Weber came in with the pitch, a fast curve, and this boy hit a hard ground ball to my left which looked like a sure hit, but I got a great jump on the ball and snagged it clean in my glove, and as I was falling I fired to the second baseman, who made his pivot and threw on to first. So we got a double play and won the game after all.

Jack laughed and yelled.

"Billy, you're my second baseman," he said. All those boys treated me like a brother, and Moore gave me a bottle of soda pop and a five-dollar bill, and he said now I was a pro. That night Jack took me out for a steak dinner, and he bragged about me all over Baltimore.

WE LEFT Baltimore on a Tuesday night in a chartered bus which pulled out from the Southern Hotel. Some of the players's wives and girl friends were there to see us leave. On both sides of the bus were these big signs in large red letters which said, "Jack Kelsey's All-Stars," and in slightly smaller numbers just below, "1941." It was some happy farewell. There was a photographer taking pictures. Jack asked me to pose with him and three of these girls. I still have the picture, and we were all really smiling.

It was the best time I ever had. We barnstormed through five states, playing night games in towns and cities against good semipro teams. Jack took me around on the days we weren't riding, and at night we played ball and went to sleep about one in the morning.

Luther Breen was my roommate on the trip. Aside from me, he was the youngest boy on the team. He came around with Jack and me after the other boys started to make fun of him. Fred Moore said that the trouble with Breen was that he always had something to say, particularly when nobody asked him. Breen was seventeen, and he was six feet one and one hundred seventy, with a long, bony face and a couple of scars on his chin and forehead. He had a small tattoo, a little red heart, on his right forearm. He let his hair grow very long. When Breen combed it forward, it hung down to his mouth. He looked strange, but he was a great player. Jack said he'd make the big leagues, if he didn't wind up in prison first.

Often Jack would take us to some museum for a couple of hours, and then we'd have lunch some place. In the afternoon, we'd walk around or sit in some park and take it easy, and Jack would tell stories about himself. About three o'clock we'd come back to the hotel and sit in the bar while Jack had a few drinks and smoked a cigar. Then I'd have to take a nap for about an hour so I'd be fresh for the game. When I woke up, sometimes Jack and Breen and I'd play poker for fun until five o'clock when it was time to get into our uniforms and go down for the evening meal. I loved those poker games. The dealer would choose his game and my favorite was seven-card draw. We used blue and red and white chips. If we'd been playing for money, I'd really be rich by now. Every time I won, Jack would say, "Billy, you been messing with those cards?" or something like that. But he was only kidding.

We went to a lot of places, mainly historical sites. We went to Fort McHenry in Baltimore, and up in Saratoga we visited the battlefield where "Gentleman Johnny" Burgoyne surrendered to the Americans. Up around Buffalo we walked along the Erie Canal, and on an off day in Pennsylvania, Jack took me and Breen to Gettysburg where we took a tour of the battlefield. Right at the place where Pickett made his charge we stood under a tree and looked out across the field—there was some thunder and lightning that afternoon—and a wind came up, and suddenly Breen let out a wild yell and grabbed at his chest like he'd been shot. "Help me, Billy," he said, staggering a few steps. "What's wrong with you, Breen?" Jack said. Breen said he imagined if he'd been living then he would have got it on Pickett's charge, and Jack said, "You may get it right now." Then it started to rain.

Jack was always riding Breen. He would say things like, "Now watch yourself, Breen," or "I'm sick and tired of taking crap from you," or "You keep crapping around, Breen, and I'll send you home in an ambulance." Jack caught Breen smoking in a phone booth in Allentown almost right after he'd promised to quit, and he nearly sent him back to High Point right then. Jack told Johnny

Hart, one of our players, that you had to hold a tight rein on a kid like Breen or he'd try to walk all over you. Maybe he was right. I don't know.

BY THE TIME we swung south and came into Washington, we had played twenty-three games and won all but two. We lost a close game to a team in Trenton, New Jersey, and got shut out in Allentown.

Every five days, Jack posted the batting averages on the door of his room. On the last sheet, I was hitting .344. Fred Moore was leading at .412. Breen was hitting .330 and leading in triples.

Coming into Washington, we were so tired we nearly collapsed in our rooms at the Dodge Hotel. We'd been riding the bus for eight hours straight, after playing four games in three days. But even so, it was exciting to see Washington for the first time. Our hotel wasn't too far from the Capitol, and the dome was all lit up the night we came in.

We'd really been looking forward to Washington. Jack had been telling us about the different sights he'd show us there. And we were going to play the Northern Virginia All-Stars in a night game at Griffith Stadium. Some local promoters had got us the stadium. It was our last game.

Early the next morning, Jack and Breen and I had a big breakfast in the hotel, and then we walked over to Union Station, which was nearby, and hired a car. It was very warm and sticky out. In a large fountain near the station, some colored boys were splashing around.

For a while we just drove without getting out of the

car, and Jack pointed things out. He wanted us to get the feel of the city. Several times he got a little confused. He called one building the Treasury Department which according to a sign was the Department of the Interior, and he called the War Department the Bureau of Printing. But there are so many buildings that it's impossible to have all the names straight.

We crossed the Memorial Bridge into Virginia, and went to the Arlington Cemetery, saw the Tomb of the Unknown Soldier and the changing of the guard. The Lee mansion was on the hill overlooking the cemetery, but we didn't go inside.

We saw the Lincoln Memorial, and we went to the top of the Washington Monument. From there we could see the entire city of Washington and some of Virginia and Maryland.

Jack didn't want us to knock ourselves out. We had to play a game that night. So after we went through the Capitol—Congress wasn't in session—Jack decided to take us over to the Smithsonian Institute where we'd just take our time wandering through it. The Smithsonian is sort of in a little park—these red buildings set among trees and open ground.

We saw the Wright plane and the *Spirit of St. Louis.* Jack told us about Lindbergh flying to Paris with just a couple of sandwiches. "He was the Lone Eagle," Jack said, and Breen really liked that part. Then we saw a French Spad which had two wings and a machine gun mounted in the rear cockpit. Then after we saw some old cars, Jack said he had to leave us.

"I got some important business," he said.

It was about one in the afternoon. We walked Jack outside to the car. It was really hot, even though there was a fair breeze.

"You take a nap, Billy," Jack said. He wanted me to get my rest.

He gave us some money for lunch and taxi fare back to the hotel. He told Breen to look out for me, and then he got in his car and drove off, waving his panama hat out the window.

"So long, you old bastard," Breen said, when Jack's car was a block away.

We had lunch in a small cafeteria on Pennsylvania Avenue. I was feeling a little tired, and Breen had a headache. I didn't eat too much, just a sandwich and a coke, but Breen had a hot turkey sandwich and two desserts. All during lunch, Breen kept telling me what an old bastard Jack was, and then he said, "I guess Jack had real important business."

"I guess so," I said.

Breen laughed.

"You sure are dumb, Billy."

"How come?"

"Never mind," Breen said, smiling.

After lunch we went into a drugstore where Breen bought some cigarettes and some aspirin for his headache. He tried to get a glass of water at the fountain so he could take his aspirin, but this boy behind the counter said he didn't have time just to serve glasses of water. There was nobody even sitting at the counter. Breen had a few words with that boy, and then he chewed up the aspirin as we walked out.

A little later we went into this place called Nichol's

Cafe, and Breen tried to buy a bottle of beer, but the waiter wouldn't serve him unless he could prove he was eighteen, and he asked for Breen's driver's license. "I didn't come here to drive a car," Breen said, acting surly, and we walked out.

We ambled along and ended up on Ninth Street, right outside the Gayety Burlesque house. There were these large posters showing these girls with hardly anything on. Breen wanted to go in, and it was all right with me, but they wouldn't sell us any tickets.

"Let's go back to the Smithsonian, Breen," I said, but he said he didn't want to go to any museum. He was in a fairly bad mood.

We walked back to the park near the Washington Monument, and we sat down under a tree on the edge of this empty field. Breen half closed his eyes and smoked a cigarette. While we were sitting there, this colored boy came running across the field, trying to get a kite off the ground. The kite took off and started to rise, and this boy kept coming, just flying.

"Breen, look at him go," I said.

Breen pushed himself up and leaned back on his elbows. "Hell, Billy, it's just a little nigger," he said. I told Breen that didn't mean that boy couldn't run, and he just made a face; and then he smiled like he suddenly got an idea, and he asked me if I thought I could whip that colored boy—he was about my size—and I told Breen that I was in Washington to play ball and not act crazy like him. He gave me this look and said I was yellow. I told Breen to have it his own way and leave me alone. I don't have anything against colored boys.

When that boy got a little closer, Breen cupped his

hands to his mouth and yelled, "Hey, you dumb little nigger. My friend here says he can whip you." I told that boy to go on, that I didn't say that; but Breen kept pushing me and trying to start something, and I kept yelling to that colored boy to just go on, that I didn't want to fight him, and he finally just walked away, looking a little scared and confused. Breen was in a worse mood than ever. I almost felt sorry for him.

"Come on, Breen," I said. "Let's get some coffee."

He sat there with his legs wide apart and his head bowed. Then he looked up and blew some smoke rings. He wouldn't talk to me though. Finally, he said, "Billy, I thought you were my friend."

"I am your friend, Breen."

"Well, no friend of mine ever sided with a nigger," he said. He got to his feet and brushed himself off, and then we walked away.

I bought him a cup of coffee at a White Tower, and he put a lot of sugar and cream in his cup. He was feeling better. He kept looking in the mirror behind the counter and smiling at himself. He was really ugly.

"Well, how is the Lone Eagle?" I said.

"Hey, Billy, you watch me tonight," Breen said.

"What for?" I said.

"I'm really going to sting that ball."

"Since when?" I said.

And we really laughed. Breen was a great player, so he knew I was only kidding.

We finally ended up in Lafayette Park across the street from the White House. There was a statue of Andrew Jackson sitting on a horse and waving his hat. There were all these pigeons on the walks.

It was about two thirty in the afternoon. We sat on a bench and took it easy. Breen smoked and made these smart remarks. Every time some girl passed, he'd say things like, "Oh, baby, I like your walk," and "Look at that, Billy, did you see that?"

After a while, Breen started in on Jack again, about what an old bastard he was, and how Breen was really happy that the last game was coming up, so he'd never have to play for Jack again. I didn't say anything.

"You think Jack's so great, don't you?" Breen said.

"I think Jack's fine, Breen," I said.

"Poor old Billy," he said. "He can't turn around without asking Jack."

We didn't say anything for a while, and then Breen said, "I wonder where Jack is now."

I told Breen that he heard Jack say he had business, and that he probably had to see the promoters; and Breen's eyes got real bright, and he shook his head. "You're so dumb, Billy," he said, and then he pulled a piece of paper out of his pocket. "That's where Jack is," he said, handing it to me. There was an address written on the paper, and I asked Breen what that all meant. He grabbed the paper out of my hand; he put his hands over his eyes and smiled real wide.

"Everybody knows but you."

"Knows what?" I said.

And then Breen started laughing again, throwing his head back.

I asked Breen where Jack was, and he suddenly pounded his fist into his hand and jumped up. "He's at Miss Tanney's!" he said.

I didn't say anything.

Breen smiled wide, and he looked around to see if anyone was listening, and he leaned toward me, putting his foot on the bench.

"It's a cat house, Billy."

"So what," I said.

"What do you mean, 'so what'?" Breen said, walking around the bench. "He sure didn't have time for us this afternoon."

"He took us on plenty of sight-seeing, Breen," I said.

"But he sure couldn't this afternoon," Breen said, jumping around. Some pigeons flew up in the trees.

He said that Johnny Hart, one of our players, told him, and that Jack had fixed Johnny up with a girl that morning at Miss Tanney's.

It was about three in the afternoon. I was feeling a little tired, and I told Breen I was going back to the hotel and take a nap. I got up from the bench and started to walk away.

Breen put a hand on my shoulder.

"Let's go there, Billy," he said.

"We can't, Breen. You know that."

"We could take a look," he said.

"I don't want to. I mean, what for?"

"Hell, we'd see a cat house, Billy," Breen said.

Breen told me his plan. He wanted to stand outside, hid behind a car or lamppost, and watch Jack and those boys come out. I told Breen that was really dumb, that I wouldn't mind going to a cat house, but I sure didn't want to sneak around and spy on Jack.

"You're Jack's pet all right," Breen said, smiling.

I told Breen I'd see him later, and I started to walk away. Breen didn't stop me this time.

"Hell, I don't need you," he said.

I walked off a little ways and turned around.

"You going there, Breen?"

He was already walking in the other direction, and he kept going past the statue of Andrew Jackson. Farther on he stopped and asked directions, showing the piece of paper to a policeman, and then he half trotted out of the park.

I didn't want to go back to the hotel by myself. So I yelled, "Breen!" and ran and caught up with him.

All the way out on the bus, Breen sat there and laughed and laughed. He couldn't control himself, and he was acting so strange that I'd wished I'd gone back to the hotel.

"It's up this street here," Breen said, pointing up at a street sign. It was a lonely old neighborhood with a lot of big shade trees. There were both colored and white people walking around, though mainly colored, and Breen kept saying we were really in darktown.

After we'd walked along for a while, Breen looked at the slip of paper and then nodded at an old apartment building on the corner.

"There it is," he said, pulling at his hair. His eyes were real bright, and his mouth was open.

"It's one big cat house," I said, and we both started to laugh so hard that we had to lean against a tree. I was getting as crazy as him.

Jack's car was parked outside. There was a guidebook to Arlington Cemetery still on the front seat.

I was all for going back to the hotel, and I asked Breen to come along, since we'd seen it and there was nothing else to do; but he kept looking at the piece of paper and biting his lower lip, and finally he said there was an apartment number written on it, and that we just had to see the door to the apartment, because that was where the cat house was, and he wanted to stand outside the door and try to hear what was going on. He looked all wild and crazy. I'd seen him this way before, and I said, "Breen, that's really dumb," and then he shook his head, like he always does when I disagree with him or don't want to go along with something he wants me to do, and he said, "Billy, I always knew you were yellow," and then he talked about how I was scared to fight that colored boy, and that I was scared of Jack, and that I was his pet, and that I'd never be worth a good damn until I got some guts, and then I said, "You're just so dumb, Breen, you make me tired." He screamed at me to shut up, and then he frogged me real hard on the arm. For a few seconds the pain went all through my body, and I thought I was going to throw up. I just stood there with my hands over my eyes.

Breen started to laugh real hard and walk around in a circle. He tried to make up to me, and he kept saying, "Come on, Billy, let's shake hands."

I started back to the hotel; I was going to take a cab. Breen caught up with me, and he promised that if I went inside for a quick look at the door to Miss Tanney's he'd leave right away with me for the Dodge Hotel.

There was no one in the hallway when we entered, and it was very quiet. The building was all run down, with the paint peeling off the walls.

We heard the elevator door open, and we ducked fast through the doorway that led to the stairs. There was no paint on the walls or steps of the stairwell. It was just gray cement. The handrail was some rusted pipe. We climbed up to the fourth floor. Before we left the stairway landing, I said to Breen, "Now we just look at the door. Hear?" He grabbed my arm and pulled me through the door to the hallway.

It was shadowy. Some of the light bulbs were out. There were some dented fire extinguishers on the wall. A few buckets were stacked near a ladder which stood in the middle of the hall. We had to walk around it. There was a dirty old green rug that went the length of the hallway.

We found Miss Tanney's door. It was number 43; the numbers were made of some gray metal, and they were tacked on the door right below the mail slot. The door had a wood frame and a glass window. A black curtain on the inside of the door covered the glass.

"We've seen it, Breen. Come on," I whispered. I pulled at Breen's arm, but he shook free. He pulled some hair down to his mouth and started chewing on it.

"I don't hear nothing," Breen said.

"Damn you, Breen. Come on."

"Shut up, Billy," Breen said, loud.

I pulled at him.

"Let go!" he said.

We heard footsteps and a rustling noise from behind the door. The curtain was pulled aside a few inches, and a dark face stared out from behind the glass. I started to move out of there, but Breen grabbed me. He wouldn't let me go, and the door swung open, and there was this short, fat colored lady. She wore yellow beads around her throat and a long green dress down to her ankles. Her hair was cut short like a boy's. She just looked at us, and Breen said, "Hey, black mama."

"What you say?" she said, putting a hand over her mouth.

"You heard me," Breen said, smiling. He lit a cigarette, and then we started to walk away. I looked back at her. "So what you looking at?" she said.

"Come on," Breen said, pulling at me. As we walked around the ladder, we heard another woman's voice. "Baby Grace, what's going on?"

We turned around and saw this white woman, about sixty years old, with long white hair that hung down to her waist. She was very thin.

"What's wrong, Baby?" she said.

The colored lady frowned and pointed at us. "That trash is what's wrong," she said. "But they going, Miss Tanney."

Breen and I looked at one another.

"Come on back here!" Miss Tanney said. I don't know why we didn't run, but we walked back, going around the ladder again.

Miss Tanney narrowed her eyes. She had white powder all over her face and lips, but no rouge, and she wore a black, old-timey dress with a red handkerchief around her neck.

"What are you hanging around here for?" she said.

I just looked at Breen, and I was afraid he was going to make some smart remark, but he didn't say a word.

"Well, ain't you going to say something?" she said.

"No, ma'am," Breen said, and then he froze and turned pale. Jack came out of the doorway, smoking a cigar. He was in his bare feet, and he wore only a pair of pants held up by suspenders.

"You know them boys, Mr. Jack?" Baby Grace said.

"Yeah, I know them," Jack said.

"Well, I'm glad you do," Miss Tanney said, and she went back inside with Baby Grace.

Jack looked at us, biting down on his cigar. Then he put his hands in his pockets and looked down at his feet.

"You call this sight-seeing, Breen?" he said, finally.

Breen's lower lip began to tremble, and he said something that wasn't clear.

"What? I can't hear you, Breen," Jack said.

Breen looked down on the floor.

"Come here!" Jack yelled. Breen backed up against a wall.

"Give me those cigarettes!" Jack said. Breen handed them over.

I never saw Jack so mad. It was like I didn't know him. He looked at me. "Billy, you know what kind of place this is?" I said I knew, and Jack said, pointing at Breen, "He told you. Right?" and I said I'd figured it out for myself, and Jack yelled, "Don't lie to me!" and then suddenly without warning, he gave Breen a hard kick on the leg. "I'm going to teach you a lesson, boy!" he yelled, and Miss Tanney rushed out of the door, holding up her hands.

"For God's sake, Jack, you want the police down my back?" she said.

She pushed us all through the door. "My God," she said, and then, as we walked down this long hallway, she broke into this cackling laughter.

We came into a large room with very little light. The

blinds were pulled, and only one lamp, in the corner of the room, was turned on. There were some oriental rugs on the floor. In front of this fake fireplace were a few soft chairs and a couch, and beside the lighted lamp in the corner was a green leather chair. Fred Moore was sitting in a soft chair, his shirt unbuttoned down the front. He was smoking a cigarette and having a drink of whiskey from a regular water glass. The bottle was on the floor by the chair.

We nodded at him.

Two girls sat on the couch, in their bathrobes. They were about twenty-five. One girl was fairly heavy with long black hair. The other girl was a skinny little blonde. They were both very pale like Miss Tanney. Baby Grace stood by the couch with her arms folded. She pointed at me.

"Mr. Jack, ain't he kind of young?"

Miss Tanney clapped her hands and laughed, and the girls began to laugh, too.

"Quiet," Jack said, raising his hand. "This here is Billy." He gave me a little push, and told me to sit down. I walked over to the green leather chair and sat down.

"And this here is just a poor excuse," Jack said, his eyes half closed. "Ain't that right, Breen?"

"If you say so, Mr. Kelsey," Breen said, looking down at the floor.

"Well, I say so!" Jack yelled, and then he swung and hit Breen in the face with an open hand.

Breen covered his face with his hands, and then he quickly dropped them. His face got very red; he folded his arms across his chest and tried to make out that nothing had happened.

"What's wrong with you, Jack?" Miss Tanney said, shaking her head. "For God's sake!"

"You be quiet, Tanney. I know what I'm doing," Jack said, but he seemed a little ashamed.

Baby Grace brought in some ice wrapped in a napkin for Breen. She put it on the ledge above the fireplace. "Come on, boy. Put this on your face," she said. Breen put the ice pack over one eye which had swelled up a little.

Everybody seemed a little embarrassed.

Then Jack walked out of the room, toward the rear of the apartment.

"Well, how are you feeling, Billy?" Fred Moore said.

"Fine. How are you feeling?" I said.

When Jack returned to the living room, he was all dressed up again and smoking a fresh cigar. I watched him out of the corner of my eye, standing there with his hands on his hips, leaning forward slightly and switching his cigar from one side of his mouth to the other. He came over and put a hand on my shoulder and started talking to Fred, but I moved out from under his hand to another part of the room.

"Now what's the matter with you?" Jack said.

I didn't say anything.

"Give him an aspirin, Tanney," Jack said. I told her that I didn't need an aspirin. I took a deep breath and let the air out slowly, and then Jack asked me to step outside.

We went out in the hall. I looked down at the floor and waited for Jack to say something.

Finally, he said, "Billy, what's wrong with you?"

I didn't say anything.

"You mad because you found me in a cat house?"

"No, sir."

"Then what are you mad for?" Jack said.

"You had no call to hit Breen, Mr. Kelsey," I said.

"I should a broke Breen's neck!" Jack said, real loud. He put his hands in his pockets and walked around. "Listen here," he said. "Breen's playing tonight. I nearly sent him back to High Point."

I looked down at the floor, and Jack told me to stop sulking, and then we went back inside.

Breen was sitting in a chair, still holding the ice pack to his face, but when he saw Jack, he got up and moved back to the fireplace.

Jack looked to see that I was watching, and then he waved at Breen. Breen looked real scared.

"Forget it, Breen," Jack said, and he went over and slapped Breen on the shoulder. "Come here," he said, and he led Breen to the couch. "You sit here between Sally and Brenda."

Sally, the little blonde, said, "You can put that ice pack down. You're going to live."

Baby Grace came over and took the wet towel from Breen. Then Brenda said, "Breen, honey, you think I'm pretty?"

"Yes, ma'am," Breen said.

Everybody started laughing.

"Did you hear that!" Baby Grace said.

When the laughter died down, Breen was smiling.

While Breen sat with Sally and Brenda, Jack had a talk with Miss Tanney near the fireplace. She kept nodding, and then I heard her say, "I understand, Jack."

Jack went over to Breen and said he wanted to talk to

him. They went off in a corner, where Jack talked low to Breen and put his arm around him. Then he said, "Brenda, come on over here." Brenda got up from the couch, tightening the belt of her bathrobe, and walked over.

While they were all talking, I took a *Life* magazine out of the rack next to the chair and began to read.

I had only looked at a few pages when Jack tapped me on the shoulder.

"Let's take a walk," he said. "Come on, Billy, get up."

Out on the street, I sat down on the fender of a car while Jack walked back and forth, his hands behind his back.

After a while, he came over, straightening out the brim of his panama. "You want some ice cream?" he said. He seemed a little tired.

We walked down to the corner, to a little grocery store, and had some ice cream.

After that, we walked around. It was getting late in the afternoon. We came to a low fence and watched these kids playing in a yard, and then we walked around some more until we came to a school playground with a few sliding boards and a row of swings. We got a drink of water at a fountain there, and then we sat down on a bench under a tree. I was really tired.

When we got back to Miss Tanney's, Breen was sitting on the couch, holding Brenda's hand. She was looking through the *Life* magazine. "What say, Billy," Breen said, and Brenda looked up and said, "Billy, ain't I met you somewhere before?" Breen was smoking, but Jack didn't say anything. We sat around for just a few more minutes, and then Jack told Miss Tanney that we all had to get back to the hotel. She acted like she was really sorry to see us go, and she took my hand and said, "Let me hear from you some time." Breen didn't want to leave, but Brenda pushed him out the door.

At the hotel, Breen and I went up to our room. I lay down and went right to sleep.

Before I knew it, Breen was shaking me to get up. He put the blue canvas bag that we shared on the bed. We made sure everything was in—our gloves, sliding pads, inner socks, spikes, and all. We always carried our uniforms on clothes hangers.

Then we packed our suitcases.

In the hallway, Jack started rapping on doors, saying, "Everybody down." We left all of our stuff on the bus in front of the hotel, and then we went into the dining room and ate a light supper with the team.

On the way to Griffith Stadium, Breen didn't say a word. I looked out the window, trying to see some of the sights Jack had shown us earlier, but after ten minutes we were in an old part of town and it was just slummy.

It had clouded up, and by the time we reached the stadium, there was some thunder and a light rain. A man holding an umbrella was there to meet us and take us to the clubhouse. "Well, if it ain't the Chicago White Sox," he said.

Griffith Stadium was the first big-league park I ever saw. It was green with high light towers, and some of the lights were already on.

We went into the clubhouse and got dressed. The lockers were large enough to stand in. There were no doors, and they were more like cages than anything.

We left the clubhouse as a team, moving down a runway, our spikes tapping on the concrete, and then we moved up a ramp and climbed some steps that led to the dugout being used by the Virginia team.

They were all sitting on the bench waiting for the rain to stop.

Going behind the batting cage, we crossed the field to the third-base dugout. It was raining harder. There was a little lake on the tarpaulin that covered the infield.

We sat on the bench and watched it rain, looking at the signboards in the outfield. Music came over the loudspeakers. Some of the Virginia players leaned out of their dugout and waved to us. They wore white uniforms with VA. ALL-STARS on their shirt fronts in orange letters. Their socks were black and orange, and they wore black caps with an orange V above the peak. Our uniforms were gray. We wore blue socks with a red stripe. KELSEY'S ALL-STARS in blue lettering was on our shirt fronts. We had dark blue caps with JK in red above the peak.

Jack sat on the dugout steps and looked up at the sky. He said it was getting lighter, that it was clearing up, but it was getting worse.

About eight o'clock it started to pour, and the game was called. There were just a few hundred people in the ball park.

In the clubhouse, Jack yelled at Breen several times to hurry up, but it didn't do much good. Breen had got one sock halfway on and just sat there in a daze. He'd still be in Washington if Johnny Hart and I hadn't helped him get ready.

It rained all night on the ride south. Jack slept in the front seat behind the driver, and he was snoring away.

Breen and I sat near the front. I had an aisle seat, as it was Breen's turn to sit by the window. There were only about fifteen of us on the bus. The Maryland boys left the team in Washington—Fred Moore, Wilcey Evans, Joe Weber, Johnny Hart, Mercer Childreth, and a few others. The rest of us were going as far as Richmond on the bus, as Jack lived there and he decided to charter it to his home. So in that way we went south together, going our separate ways from Richmond.

Most everyone was sleeping. I tried to sleep, but I couldn't get comfortable, and after a while I looked over at Breen. He was smoking, and his face was lit up ever so slightly from the headlights of the passing cars; I tried to talk to him, but he wouldn't say anything, and then I noticed that he was crying. There were a few tears sliding down. "What's the matter?" I said. Breen took a drag on his cigarette and wiped his eyes with the back of his hand, and he said, "Billy, why don't you be quiet?" and I said, "There are plenty of girls in High Point, Breen," and he half laughed and coughed, and he said, "Jesus, you're really crazy."

I was really feeling great to be going home.

Later that night, we pulled into a roadhouse on the way to Richmond, and we had hamburgers and coffee. Jack and a few of the boys ordered some drinks, and after the meal, Jack raised his glass and said, "Well, boys, the season's over."

Rock Creek

As THEY were about to leave, Chou began jumping and barking. John put his hand to his face; he had forgotten to do his exercises with the weighted shoe—a red steel shoe with a bar and weight attachment. He felt he had better do the exercises while he had the energy. Lately he was always tired, but he would be particularly tired when he came home. So he put the leash down on the chair in the hall and went into his bedroom and tied the shoe—it weighed about twelve pounds—to his foot, and then, sitting in a chair, he began to bend and straighten his leg; he would start out with his leg hanging down in a normal position, and then he would raise it horizontal to the floor and hold it stiffly for as long as he could stand it. He repeated this about thirty times. It was to strengthen his knee and thigh. The muscles had atrophied badly, and his leg was quite weak. Chou, sitting in the doorway, watched him; she barked at him from time to time. She was irritated and confused. He'd promised to take her out, and now he was delaying again, and she probably wouldn't get to go.

Chou was John's mother's dog, a gray, long-faced toy

poodle with sad eyes. She was three years old. Since he had come back from the hospital, they had spent quite a lot of time together in the house and had become dependent on each other for company. But for Chou, and Bessie, the maid, who worked days, he was alone. His parents were in Europe and his sister was away at school. Chou followed him everywhere. While he ate in the dining room, she would remain at his feet under the table. If he read the paper in the living room, she would jump up beside him on the chair. She hated to be alone, and he welcomed her company. They had a game. When she wanted to play, she would approach his chair with a small, yellow woollen cat in her mouth. He would take the cat and toss it across the room, and she'd streak off and pounce on it, slamming it from side to side on the floor, then, crouching, look at him. "Chou, bring it back," he'd say, but she would run into one bedroom or another with the cat in her mouth, crawl under a bed, and wait for him to find her. The game was more hide-and-seek than retrieving. It gave her a great deal of excitement and pleasure, and she never tired of it. But after twenty minutes of looking under beds, he was too exhausted to go on, and he would have to go to his room and lie down for an hour. She would lie at his feet.

He had broken his leg in two places. The cast, which had gone above his knee, had now been off for ten days. He had worn it for three months. Aside from the itching under the cast, he had not been in great discomfort or pain.

"Come on, Chou," he said, untying the weighted shoe. He didn't really want to take her, but he felt sorry for her. He knew she wanted to go into the fields and woods.

Between the time his parents had gone to Europe and he had come home, Chou had been boarded in a kennel outside Washington, and after she was brought back to the house, she had never got to go out but for two brief walks a day with Bessie, a tall, hefty, mocha-brown-skinned Negro, who invariably said to her, "Let's go, Chou. Do your business. I got my work to do." Bessie called her a "little garbage hustler." Chou would often dawdle with Bessie until she had got her ration of smells. "Aw, come on, honey," Bessie would say. "We ain't got all day."

Chou had been angry with him earlier in the week when he had gone out several times and left her behind. He had feared the responsibility, and anyway he had wanted to take a drive and be alone. If he took her, something could always happen. He was afraid that somehow he'd lose her, that she would run away and he would not ever find her again. Little things upset him; he needed all of his energy to concentrate on his driving. But when he drove into Alexandria, knowing that she dearly loved it there, he had felt cruel and sorry—though he desperately wanted to be alone.

When he returned, instead of the wild greeting he had come to depend on, she had looked annoyed, and ignored him. It was strange how much he depended on her. When he wasn't with her, he thought about her, trying to give his mind something to hold on to. She was a little mystery to him. Anything out of the ordinary offended her, and she was very unfriendly toward strange-looking people or very old people, and there was one sadly retarded girl that she had barked at with great anger one morning when the girl had tried to pet her.

Children loved her, and she endured them. While they played with her, she would sometimes look at him as if to say, "You never please me, but can't you at least make them go away?" He was very fond of her—of her sad eyes and strange moods.

JOHN PUT ON a brown sport coat with a rip in the elbow. Under the coat, he wore a blue sweater over a faded blue shirt with a frayed collar. He looked out the window. The day was sunny and clear—a fine autumn day in Washington. He always preferred the autumn, and normally the blue crispness of the day would have filled him with delight. But he was tired and despondent, and he was going out mainly for Chou. She was panting to go. He wore an old pair of gray pants with a tear in the knee. These were the pants he had worn on the day, three months before, when he'd broken his leg. He had been walking on a trail in Rock Creek Park, high above a ravine, and then, while climbing up a rocky ledge overlooking the ravine, he had suddenly fallen. Later, in the hospital, he felt that he'd just lost his concentration, that he had been too careless, but it troubled him that he couldn't remember whether he'd just slipped, whether some loose rock had given way, or whether he had just stepped out and found nothing there. It hadn't been a bad fall—the slope was not, after the first fifteen feet, steeply graded, and some trees broke his pitching, rolling descent—and he would have been all right but for a few bruises and scratches had it not been for his collision with a fallen tree trunk at the bottom. He had lain there in considerable pain for two hours in a soft bed of leaves, until a woman on horseback came along a bridle path above the trail and saw him. An hour later, he was carried out of the park on a stretcher and placed in an ambulance.

A week before the fall, two of his oldest and closest friends, Ewing and Hal, had been killed in North Carolina in a nighttime automobile accident. John was supposed to have gone with them on the trip to Charlotte, where Ewing's girl friend was to have fixed Hal and him up with blind dates, but John had come down with a bad cold and had remained in Washington.

He picked up a book that was on his dresser and put it in the pocket of his coat. Chou jumped up on the bed, jumped down, and began to bark. He felt a little dizzy. For the last months, he'd had trouble concentrating; he had to do everything slowly. His memory was unreliable, and he was often confused. There seemed to be a weight on his head that made him want to close his eyes. He tried not to think of Ewing and Hal, of death in general, of his own death, of not being with them when they died, but he would always remember them—in a slight daze, in cold hysteria—at different times of the day. He often found it difficult to breathe. As he felt for the book in his pocket, he suddenly thought of them, and he said, with a slightly hoarse and tired voice, "Oh, Lord, I don't want to die." He looked down at Chou, and he felt he had been alone too much.

He was eighteen, about six feet tall, frail, loose and gangling, with a long face and a wide, full mouth. His expression was tentative and shy. He lit a cigarette, and then he picked up the leash from the chair in the hall. Chou was right at his heels. He said goodbye to Bessie, and he and the dog walked outside and got into his father's car. All the way to the park, Chou stood up on the seat, with her front paws on the rim of the window.

IT HADN'T RAINED for a while. When John pulled into a dirt lot, the tire ruts were deep and hard. He didn't want to get out of the car, and he sat there leaning on the steering wheel for a few minutes, with Chou pawing at the sleeve of his coat, and looked out. Beyond the lot was a grassy field, with the creek to the left of a row of trees. Farther on, there was a small tributary of the creek which divided the field from a wooded hill. Up the hill was the trail that led to the ravine where he had broken his leg. He would stay away from the trail. The day had turned faintly warm in the autumn sunlight. The trees on top of the hill were yellow and russet and brown. He got out of the car and went around it and opened the door on the other side. Chou jumped down, wagging her tail. "O.K., Chou, come on," he said. He took the leash, and they walked across the dirt lot until they came to a low wooden rail, which he stepped over; Chou went underneath.

When he stepped onto that sunny field, he felt at a loss. Chou suddenly seemed very timid, and he felt inadequate as a master. It was the first time that he had been on foot in the park since he had broken his leg. He felt strange, and he nearly got back into the car. Then, in some desperation, he swung his arm toward the empty field and said, "Run, Chou, run!" but she only stood there looking up at him, wagging her tail. She was waiting for him. The sun was in her eyes, and they were half closed and slightly watery. She had a nearsighted quality. She looked irritated. She didn't like to stand very long in one spot.

He began to walk across the field, and she followed him. He felt that she wanted him to be a certain way on their walk together, but he couldn't seem to manage it. His leg bothered him; he walked slowly and dragged it somewhat. He looked back at Chou, who was coming slowly, in her earnest little trot. She looked so small, he thought. She looked bigger in the house; here she hardly rose above the grass. In the house, though sad-eyed, she was frisky and playful, but out in the field she was quite timid and uncertain. She wasn't enjoying herself, and he felt it was his fault. "Run, Chou, run. For God's sake!" he yelled at her. She stood close to him, looking away at something, as though distracted, then gave him a quick glance. "Oh, God, leave me alone," he said. He began to walk. She dawdled behind, sniffing at the ground. His leg hurt and he wanted to sit down, and he was walking only to give her some exercise. She didn't seem interested, but he knew if he sat down on a bench she would look at him accusingly. She lingered, moving in slow half circles behind him.

When he turned around, she stopped and sat down. He told her to come on, but she wanted to go in another direction—nearer the creek, where perhaps the smells were better. It was too far; he didn't want to go that far. He called her. She looked up at him, baring her front teeth a trifle, then looked quickly in the direction of the creek. He called to her again, but she wouldn't come, and then he turned around and walked away. He knew she wouldn't go by herself. He didn't want to take her to the creek. Too much could happen there. She might have one of her wild fits, he thought. She padded along behind him, looking hurt and bewildered. He felt exasperated, and he yelled to her, "Chou, it's nothing personal! So stop acting silly!" But she only looked down at the ground, as though preoccupied with a smell or a piece of the terrain. Suddenly, she began to bark at a squirrel; she streaked across the field and chased it over the small wooden bridge that crossed the tributary. The squirrel ran up a tree, with Chou barking at it below. Chou's spirits improved. She came trotting back with her tongue out and stood up with her front paws on his knee and stretched, and he decided to take her to the creek after all.

THEY WALKED along together. Chou followed him quickly now, along a bridle path covered with fallen leaves that led under an old stone bridge to the bank of the creek. They passed an old mill. Chou could hear ducks, and she began to bark in a near frenzy. He put the leash on her, for he was afraid she might follow them into the water—something she had done the year before, he suddenly remembered, when Hal and Ewing were along. He wondered if she remembered them. Chou was straining at the leash, standing on her back legs. Quacking, the ducks quickly left the wet ground at the water's edge and paddled down the creek toward the falls. There were white ducks and mallards, green heads and speckled. Chou was disappointed. She kept barking at the ducks, but they receded farther and farther.

John watched them float downstream. Around the bend of the creek—about a mile farther on, he remembered—there was the sledding hill, a marvellous slope that Hal and Ewing and he had used during one rare snowy Washington winter. He thought of the time they had all gone down the slope on their sleds, coasting onto the ice-covered creek. They had called it the Danger Run. The idea was to test courage, to see how far out toward the thin ice they'd go before turning. Hal had gone part way through the ice. They had all been about eleven then. John and Ewing had got in trouble with Hal's mother for having persuaded him to go sledding right after he had recovered from influenza, and Hal had got wet and ruined his new coat. It seemed like such a rotten joke now, her worrying about that, he thought. He put a hand over his eyes. Chou strained on the leash, and he looked down at her; then he took a deep breath, and began to sink deeper into reverie. All sound and sight were blotted out as he stood immobile on the creekside. He could see them in his mind's eye so clearly. Ewing, always smiling and joking, had raised their spirits. Hal was very serious, almost solemn in a way, and he depended on Ewing and John to make him laugh; he was very kind and honest and dependable. They had all been just like brothers. They'd played baseball together in the various boy leagues, right up to Legion ball. Ewing was very erratic in the field and at bat, but liable to stun you with something absolutely sensational, and Hal was steady and reliable, while John, on the other hand, was a little like Ewing but not as good.

He began to think of the time when they were thirteen, and he was always in fights and regularly getting the worst of it, particularly from a boy named Allie Conroy, who was a year older. Conroy would wait for him and fight him on the playground after school. Ewing and Hal, for the sake of his honor, would never interfere, but after they had witnessed several humiliations, they took him to see a colored man named Soames Hambleton—or Hamby, as he was known. He was a tall, copper-brown-skinned man with high cheekbones. He looked a little like an Indian, and he was supposed to have been a pro fighter, but he was then working as a mechanic in a garage. They all went down to the garage and persuaded Hamby to teach John how to fight Allie Conroy. During the instruction, Ewing said, smiling, "Now, come on, Hamby, don't beat him too bad. Johnny's beat up enough all ready."

Hal was very serious through all of it. "Run through it all again, Hamby," he'd said. "Conroy's bigger and stronger and has got the reach."

Hamby was very nice. He had taught John all the moves and defenses. He had said to him, "Well, son, I'm gonna show you how to cut a bigger boy down to size, how to slip a jab and get inside and get to his body, and then when he drops his hands, how to go for his head, how to hook off a jab, and how to move away and how to move in, how to glide and shuffle, and how not to think too much about getting hurt so you won't waste your strength worrying." Later on, John had beaten Conroy badly, much to everyone's surprise, and afterward the three of them had gone down to see Hamby at the garage, and they'd had sandwiches together and celebrated. "See, you just listen to old Hamby," Hamby had said. "He's been around some."

Hamby died a year later of a heart attack. He was about sixty-five, it was thought, but Mr. Travis, the owner of the garage where he worked, said, "It's hard to tell the age of a colored man. They don't age like white people." He and Hal and Ewing wanted to go to the funeral. Mr. Travis said he'd let them know about the arrangements. Hal's mother thought it wasn't right for white boys to go to a colored man's funeral—a man that didn't work for you. The colored people, she said, wouldn't like it—they'd resent it. But John and the two others disagreed with her, for, as Ewing said, "Hamby wouldn't mind, and that's all that really matters." It turned out, as far as they knew, that Hamby didn't even have a funeral. Mr. Travis told them that Hamby's "nephew or someone" claimed the body at the hospital and had him buried on practically the same day, but he didn't know where. It seemed that Hamby had no family, really—that his wife had run off about twenty years before and his children, grown now, were probably somewhere in Detroit. "Well, he sure was one fine colored man," Mr. Travis had said, and they had certainly agreed.

WHEN THESE impressions stopped, John felt very strange and light, as though he were still fourteen. He felt disoriented, and had to stand there awhile to get his bearings. Chou was a small, gray blur at first, but gradually became clear. She was lying on her stomach patiently watching the creek. He hoped he could concentrate on her and not think about anything else. Thinking of the past confused and frightened him. It upset him to drift away like that and then come back feeling strange and lost. He thought if he could just keep his mind on her, he'd be all right. Chou put her front paws on his knees. The ducks had left for good. On the way back to the field, he let her chase some squirrels. By the time they passed the mill near the bridge, she was thoroughly hot and tired and thirsty. Her tongue was hanging out, and her eyes were almost completely closed. He told her, "O.K., Chou. We'll get some water." He had a slight desire to go into the old mill, to see what it would be like to stand there again; he had played there when he was a boy. The plaque on the outside of the mill said it was built in 1801. But he passed up going inside. He and Chou went across the lot to the car to see if her spare dish was there, but he couldn't find it. Then they walked across again to a small stone drinking fountain. He tried the spigot that extended from the base, but it didn't work. Then he cupped his hands and filled them with water from the drinking spout and stooped down and offered the water to Chou. She didn't want any. "Damn it, Chou, come on," he said. The water leaked out through his hands, and he stood up and got a drink himself; then he refilled his hands with water and kneeled down again. She took a little, licking his hand, but most of the water leaked out again.

He was very tired. His leg hurt. It had been fairly warm, but the sun had dropped low in the sky; there were many long shadows now, and there was a cool breeze. He wanted to sit down and rest, and he walked to a bench that was still in the sun. Chou trotted along beside him. She was in a wonderful mood, very alert and serene. He sat down on the bench—a rough-slatted picnic bench—and lit a cigarette. Then he put the leash on Chou, who sat at his feet, and looped it around his arm.

He pulled the book out of the side pocket of his coat. He had bought the book in a drugstore that morning—

he didn't really know why. It was called *Suicide in Scandinavia.* He thought he was curious about the suicidal state of mind. He flipped through the pages, reading at random. Chou sat quietly, looking up at him occasionally. He read some case histories of suicides and became quite despondent. Oh, God, he thought, I hope I never get that low; I don't want to die. After a while, he closed his book, putting his hands over his eyes. "Jesus, I hope I never kill myself," he said out loud. He began to feel very warm and strange, and his heart began to beat rapidly. He tried to stand up, but he fell back down on the bench. "Oh, damn it to hell! The hell with it," he said. A shudder passed through him. He thought of Ewing and Hal. If you could die that way, just out one day and gone, then what was the point of living? He began to breathe hard, and, after a kind of convulsion, he turned his back on Chou and put his arms on the back of the bench. He shut his eyes very tight, then opened them and stared at the sleeve of his coat. Gradually, his breathing became calmer, until it appeared to be so even and regular that he scarcely seemed to be breathing at all. Their deaths had finally registered. It was true. They were dead forever.

AFTER NEARLY half an hour, John raised his head and turned around. He wondered if anyone had seen him, but the park was empty. It was very quiet except for the sound of an occasional car going across the bridge over the creek, the "caw, caw" of a crow, and the sound of leaves blowing across the grass. He'd go out and see them tomorrow, he thought. They were in different cemeteries, at opposite ends of town, and he would start out early in the morning.

He sat there and looked at the woods. Chou was anxious to go home. She put her paws on his knees and, yawning, looked toward the car. Leaning forward, he took her leash off and yelled, "Run, Chou, run!" and she ran off in a streak, cutting sharply to the right and throwing herself into a pile of leaves, then jumping up and shaking them off. She rolled on the grass, then jumped up and went after a squirrel again. "Come on!" he called. Eagerly, she ran back to him. He put the leash on her, and they began to walk to the car. After a few steps, he turned around and looked at the park again. The field was in a gray, dusky light. Farther on, the woods were in darkness; he couldn't make out the trees. He smelled leaves burning. He could see the light of a small fire and a man with a rake. He looked down at Chou and thought, She's a very honest little dog. When she knows I'm leaving for school, she'll ignore me. When she sees my suitcase, it's all over. She won't grieve. He thought there was no one better at hello and poorer at goodbye.

When John opened the door, Chou jumped right up on the seat. He started the car, and as he drove across the bridge, Chou stood up at the window for a final look at the creek, which, in the fast-fading light, could hardly be seen.

The Boy Who Used Foul Language

IT WAS EARLY in the morning, in Washington, late in the winter of 1940, and gray light was coming through the bedroom window. John sat up in bed, looking very pale, wearing a blue bathrobe over his cotton pajamas. A white towel was wrapped around his neck and covered his chest. He licked his lips and took a deep breath. He needed a haircut badly. It was his sixth week of convalescence after contracting pneumonia in both lungs. His face and body were thin, and though normally a slender boy, he had not regained the weight lost in his illness. Bessie, a large, gentle Negro woman who had been working for his family since before he was born, had told him that he had nearly died. "You was some poor little rip," Bessie had said. "But you going to be fine now, honey." He was ten years old. He lay back and looked at the ceiling. Oh well, he thought, he wasn't dead, and, as Ewing would say, a miss was as good as a mile. Ewing was one of his two best friends. His other best friend was Hal.

Nobody was up. He felt like calling Bessie, who was sleeping outside his room on a little cot in the hall.

Though she had other duties, she had been his nurse. He wanted to call her, or ring the small dinner bell on the table by his bed, but there was nothing particular that he wanted. After a while, he got out of bed, put on some white athletic socks that were on the floor, and then went out in the hall to see Bessie. She was sound asleep, lying on her side. Her mouth was open and she was snoring slightly. She was too big for the cot. He thought if she just moved once she'd fall out and wake the whole house. There was a red bandanna around her head. She was covered up to her throat by an old green coverlet. Her clothes, along with her bathrobe, were across the back of a broken card chair. On the seat of the chair was an alarm clock and her glasses.

"Hey, Bessie," John whispered. He knelt down and said into her ear, "You're so nice and brown." He smiled. It was something he'd heard her boy friend, Hampton Archibald, say to her when he had come to the house one night to take her home. She didn't move. Downstairs, the chimes of the grandfather clock sounded six times. She didn't have to get up until seven.

John went back into his room and picked up a book that was on the floor. Then he sat cross-legged on the bed and began to read. He was three quarters through the book. From time to time, he would stop reading and look at the colored illustrations. He loved to look at them, and he thought the book was one of the best he had ever read. It was *Treasure Island.* He read for a half hour, and then, feeling a little cold, closed the book and got back under the covers and listened to the wind against the windows. Lying there under a pale-blue quilt, he could hear a shutter banging against a nearby house. The room was washed with gray light. He thought about the book. It made him happy and sad at the same time. He lay very quietly and concentrated on the sound of the wind.

Sunlight came into his room. He got up out of bed and looked out the window. The wind was blowing the clouds away. Some of the trees were bending slightly in the wind. The chimes of the clock sounded seven. Almost at the same time, Bessie's alarm clock began to ring. "Hey, Bessie," John yelled. He went out into the hall. Bessie was reaching over and turning off the alarm. She sighed and put on her glasses.

"Oh, Bessie, you're so nice and brown," John said, smiling.

Bessie laughed, rubbing her eyes. "How you feel, honey?" she said.

"Fine," John said. "I feel all better."

"Uh-huh," she said, sitting up and putting her robe around her. "Well, you ain't supposed to get careless, now."

"Will you make me some pancakes?" John asked.

"Uh-huh," Bessie said.

"With plenty butter and syrup."

"O.K."

"Hal and Ewing are coming today," he said.

"Yeah? I thought they coming next week," Bessie said, teasing him a little.

John smiled. He was really looking forward to seeing them. It was the first day he'd been allowed visitors since he became sick.

Bessie straightened her bed, picked up her clothes from the chair, and started down to her bathroom in the basement. She told John that she would bring his breakfast as soon as she could. She had to start getting his sister, Carol, and his father taken care of first. His father had an early appointment, and his sister would be going to school. His mother was still asleep.

"Now, you be here when I get back," Bessie said.

"You better hurry up," John said, watching her go down the stairs. He heard her half singing, half humming, until she went through the door to the basement.

He went back into his room and sat on his bed. He thought he heard some birds singing. Feeling excited, he went over to a window and opened it. A strong gust of cold air hit him in the chest. He couldn't hear the birds. Still, he thought there was a spring smell in the air, and his hands felt warm in the sun on the window sill. After listening a little longer, he closed the window and got back into bed. Maybe he was just imagining it about spring, he thought. His father said that he was always imagining things the way he wanted them to be.

Before leaving for school, his sister stopped in his room. She was twelve, slightly gangling, with a wide mouth, like his own, and green eyes that were playful and somewhat furious at the same time. Her hair was long and brown. She wore a red sweater and gray skirt and brown-and-white saddle shoes. Carrying her schoolbooks and a tan coat, she looked at him with her head slightly cocked to one side. "Don't fall out of bed, you silly thing," she said.

He sighed, then looked at the ceiling, then looked at her.

"Aren't you going to say anything?" she asked.

"No," John said.

She shook her head. "I just wanted to tell you, there's no pancakes left. Bessie spilled the batter on the floor."

John glowered. She'd better be lying, he thought.

"Oh, don't look at me that way," she said, and ran out laughing.

He heard her run down the stairs. She was really stupid, he thought. He didn't like her to call him a silly thing, and she knew it. Last summer, she had said, "Oh, John, you are just so silly all the time. Everybody says so, and Mother and Daddy agree." He had got angry, turned red, and called her a little bitch. She had cried and told their mother, who slapped him in the face, forced him to apologize, and made him promise never to use such language again.

While he lay there wondering whether Carol was telling the truth about the pancakes, he heard his father come up the stairs. John quickly got out of bed, combed his hair in front of the mirror above his bureau, then got back in bed just as his father came through the door. He was ready to leave, wearing his brown topcoat and gray fedora. He was carrying a large brown envelope and the morning papers. "Hi, boy," he said.

John broke into a wide smile, then looked a little distant. "Hi, Daddy," he said. He wanted to appear nonchalant, as Ewing would say.

His father laid the newspapers on the bed. "There's a good story on Cecil Travis. He's looking good in spring training," he said. "But don't you start thinking we'll win the pennant."

John nodded, started to say something, but suddenly became confused.

"Well, you get better, now. I'm taking you to the opener," his father said. He patted John on the head. "I'll see you," he said.

"See you, Daddy," John said, smiling slightly.

His father looked so fresh and wide awake and in such a good humor that John wished he could have stayed longer. He loved it when his father was in a good mood. They'd have a fine time together then. He liked it when his father kidded around, like when he called him Wrong-Way Corrigan. When his father was not in a good mood, he would call him "stubborn" and "contrary" and a "boy who does everything ass-backwards," and things that were much worse. Lately, his father had been very patient, trying to explain everything, saying that he should not be so "extreme" all the time and not insist so that he "loved this" and "loved that" and "hated this" and "hated that," that he should be more "moderate." They had been getting along very well, John thought. He hadn't been whipped since he'd been sick; he hadn't even been yelled at.

BESSIE BROUGHT John's breakfast. He sat up in bed and she put the tray on his lap, but then he decided he wanted to eat on the little table that stood by the window. Bessie removed some books and his baseball glove from the table and then brought the table over by his bed.

"Well, I hope you like it, honey," Bessie said. There were pancakes, with maple syrup and butter, and orange juice and a glass of milk. John smiled and nodded. "Say, hand me my baseball glove," he said.

"Why, you going to eat it for breakfast?"

"Oh, please just hand it here, Bessie," he said.

She handed him the glove. He wanted it in bed with him. It reminded him that he was getting better.

He told Bessie to pull up a chair. "Let's talk," he said, cutting into his pancakes with a fork.

"Boy, I got work to do."

"Oh, you just sit down," John said.

She brought his desk chair over near the table and sat down.

There was nothing particular that he wanted to say, but he just wanted to be near her for a while. It was the last time she would stay the night, as he was well enough now to do without her. She was going back to her own children—Yancy, a girl of thirteen, and Simpson, who was seven. John knew them. Bessie brought them with her sometimes.

"Say, how do you spell 'spinach'?" John asked.

"Now, ain't you something," she said, frowning.

"Oh, come on, let's hear you spell it," he said.

"It don't matter that I can't spell it," she said. At least I understands what it mean."

"How do you spell 'asparagus'?" John asked.

She smiled. "I going to get me a peach-tree switch and tan you," she said.

"Bessie, are you really going home tonight?" he asked.

"Honey, I got to." She stood up and picked up his schoolbooks from his desk. "Your mama say you got to start doing your back work today," she said, putting the book on his bed.

John immediately pushed them onto the floor.

"Now, that ain't nice," Bessie said, taking his tray from the table. "You just going to pick them up by yourself."

Bessie left the room with the tray.

John propped some pillows against the headboard of the bed, then leaned back and picked up one of the morning papers. He went right to the sports page to find the story on Cecil Travis. It was wonderful. Cecil was his hero, his favorite player in the American League. He knew all about him—that his middle name was Howel, that he was from Riverdale, Georgia, and was born August 8, 1913, that he had hit .344 in 1937 in a hundred and thirty-five games, his best season up to then, and exactly how he looked at the plate and in the field. The story didn't add too much, except for some predictions about the coming season and what Cecil had done during the winter, but still John found it fascinating. There was one part, where Clark Griffith was quoted as saying, "Cecil moves like a big cat, he's so graceful out there," that nearly made him tremble. He loved that. He would try to move like a big cat, too. He read the story three times.

ABOUT AN HOUR later, John began to yell, "Bessie! Bessie!"

Bessie was in the basement and couldn't hear him, but his mother appeared. She was a nervous, pretty woman in her mid-thirties, of a slight-medium build, with auburn hair and green eyes a shade darker than his sister's. Fresh and scented, she wore a pale-blue dress and held in her right hand a pack of cigarettes and a nickel-plated lighter. "What's the matter, John?" she asked.

"Nothing."

"What are you calling Bessie for?" she asked. "Can I help you?"

"No, I just want to see Bessie about something."

His mother looked faintly annoyed. "She's washing clothes in the basement," she said. "How are you feeling?"

"Fine," he said.

She closed her eyes briefly and sighed, then lit a cigarette and inhaled deeply. John began to cough and wave his hand in front of his face.

"Oh, will you stop that!" his mother said. "What are you hiding under the covers?"

"Nothing. Oh please, may I see Bessie?" he said.

"Are you going to play some joke on her?"

"No."

"She has no time to be bothered, and you're very cruel to her."

"I am not," John said.

"She's a human being."

"Oh, I know that," John said.

"She's going to have to walk up three flights of stairs," his mother said. "You really ought to be ashamed of yourself." She smoothed her hair and left the room.

John smiled. He couldn't wait to see Bessie. He had been reading Blackstone's *Modern Card Tricks and Secrets of Magic.* There was hardly anything he would rather do than fool her.

Bessie came in looking a little weary, rubbing her forehead. John sat up in bed and pulled a deck of cards from beneath the covers. He was in a state of great excitement. "Bessie, take a card, any card," he said. "No, wait a second. Turn around."

"Now, ain't you some boy? You know I got my work to do. If your mama saw me messing around and—"

"Sh-h-h. Turn around, Bessie."

"I come all the way up here and you say, 'Turn around.' It ain't much of a trick if I got to turn around." She sighed and turned around.

John reviewed something in the book and examined the cards. "O.K. Take a card, Bessie."

"Ain't you going to shuffle them?"

"I already have," John said, turning slightly red.

"Hmm!" she said, taking a card. "It the four of diamonds."

"Oh, don't *tell* me, Bessie. You sure are stupid."

She sighed. "Now, honey, that ain't nice," she said.

"Oh, you're so *silly*. You've just *ruined* it," he said, looking toward the door. It was wide open. "Now, you hurry and take another card, and keep your voice down," he said in a half whisper.

"O.K.," she said, taking a card.

He took it from her, keeping it face down, then he carefully put it in the deck, which he awkwardly cut in a prearranged way. He began to count silently, down from the top of the deck, and then pulled a card from the middle somewhere.

"Your card was the jack of hearts," John said, looking at her intently.

"Uh-uh," Bessie said, shaking her head.

"It was too!" John said.

"Honey, the card I pick is the king of diamonds."

John got very red in the face and began to cough. He had done it perfectly three times before she'd come in, and now he'd messed it up.

Bessie brought a pitcher of water and a glass from the table. "You better come out from under your spell. Come on, take a drink of water," she said.

"No. You can drink it," John said.

"I ain't sick, John. You the one who sick."

"I'm not sick. Why don't you go home?" he said.

His mother suddenly walked through the open door. She looked at the cards on the bed, at John, then at Bessie, who was still holding the glass of water. "Bessie, I don't pay you to watch card tricks," she said.

"No, Ma'am."

"I knew you'd bother her," his mother said to John.

"He ain't bothering me," Bessie said, looking down.

"Now, you be quiet and get on with the wash."

"Yes, Ma'am."

"Oh, why can't Bessie rest some?" John said.

"I've had just about enough out of you," his mother said.

Bessie put the glass of water on the night table and slowly walked out of the room. John took a deep breath, then looked down at the cards on the blue quilt. His mother stood quietly in the center of the room, pressing her fingers against her temples and slowly moving her head from side to side.

John took a deep breath, turned red, and said, "Bessie's no slave. Lincoln freed the slaves."

"Oh, she's been *talking* to you! You just believe everything she says," his mother said.

"It's true," John said. "And she gets low wages."

"Now, you just be quiet," she said. "I'm going to talk to Daddy about your insolence."

"I don't care," John said.

"I do not like your tone of voice, John. It's very disagreeable," she said. "Between you and Bessie, I'm going out of my mind. Why, she's as bad as you—so surly, and she never smiles anymore. Why, she doesn't even say 'Good morning.' One of these days, I'm going to say, 'Bessie, you just get out and keep walking.' "

"Then I'm going, too," John said.

"Oh, really!"

"I sure am," John said.

"You've become a *very* difficult boy," she said, shaking her head. "When I took care of you, you were so nice and *appreciative,* so pleasant to be with. I'd give you a bath and tell you a story, and you'd smile and—" She bit her lip. "You were so sweet and *loyal.*"

John made a face, then closed his eyes.

"Oh, look at you!" she said. "No wonder they threw you out of school."

"Well, I'm back in," John said.

"No thanks to you."

She shook her head, put her hands over her eyes, and left the room.

AFTER JOHN had been alone for ten minutes, he picked up his geography book from the floor, and, opening it at random, began to read about the Glacier National Park in Montana. It was fairly interesting, he thought. There was a photograph of some men and women on horseback. The riders were sitting quietly on their horses in a little clearing. There was a tent in the clearing and smoke rising from a campfire. Behind the tent were tall pine trees, and rising up beyond the trees was a snowy mountain. After a while, he looked with resentment at his assignment sheet. He had to read a chapter on irrigation projects and annual rainfall in Nebraska. He read a few pages of that, then slammed the book shut and threw it onto the floor. It made him unhappy to read something that Miss Dornholder had assigned. Miss Dornholder was his fifth-grade teacher, and he hated her. His father had told him that she was a human being like anyone else and deserving of his sympathy and respect. But what did his father know about her? He wished Miss Dornholder would retire. She was certainly old enough, he thought. He saw her in his mind's eye, beside the blackboard, wearing a long blue dress with a small cameo brooch pinned on the front of it. She was standing there on heavy legs, with a severe, unpleasant expression on her face. Suddenly, he heard her yelling at him. "How dare you use foul language!"

He lay there feeling warm and angry; perspiration formed on his upper lip. He didn't use foul language so much, he thought—only occasionally in the playground. He had never directed any foul language at her. But she had overheard him sometimes. He and Ewing occasionally used foul language, but Hal never did. Hal was wonderful. He didn't have an enemy in the world. Everybody liked and respected him. But Ewing and I aren't so well liked, John thought. "They either like us a lot or not at all," Ewing had said. It was true.

John felt very warm and feverish thinking about Miss Dornholder. He picked up his baseball glove and pounded the pocket. Hal hardly ever even got angry, but when he did you had better watch out. He was a wonderful fighter. John wished he could be that way, even-tempered and pleasant and well-liked. Lying on his bed, he threw his glove up in the air. It landed behind the bed, caught between the headboard and the wall. Angrily, he got out of bed, and managed to move the bed enough to retrieve his glove. Then he kicked the books that were on the floor and threw himself back on the bed.

He closed his eyes. Gradually, he saw his mother. She was standing in the school playground—it was three months before—wearing her fur coat. It was after school. The day was cold and clear. Miss Dornholder had asked John's mother to meet her on the playground, as her room was being used by the Cooking Club. "Well, I want to say I'm very unhappy with your son, John," she had begun, looking at him, and then had gone on to say how troublesome and unpleasant he had been—how his handwriting was poor, and how his language had been so unutterably foul on occasion that she was unable then to repeat the words, and that if he continued in his present manner he would no doubt end up in a reformatory. All during Miss Dornholder's high-pitched condemnation of him, he had been distracted by the strange, attentive tilt of his mother's head. He had thought she was trying so hard to be friendly and pleasant. She had stood there with the collar of her fur coat turned up, nodding, smiling, looking serious, nervous, and slightly dazed, as if to say, "If you only keep him in school, I'll agree with anything." He had wanted to laugh, but had controlled himself. Now, in bed, he suddenly laughed until the tears came.

He was getting hungry. Bessie would be bringing his

lunch soon, he thought. He hoped she would remember to make him a grilled-cheese sandwich. He had asked her for it the day before, but he had forgotten to remind her. His mind wandered over all the lunches she had ever made for him. The lunches at home were better than the lunches he ate at school, even though Bessie made them. He could never take a grilled-cheese sandwich to school. It was no good cold. Bessie often made him bacon-lettuce-and-tomato sandwiches for school. She also made him sliced-chicken sandwiches and bologna, liverwurst, turkey, and ham sandwiches. Sometimes she'd put in a roll with pieces of cold fried chicken. He liked that more than anything else, except for the American grilled cheese. She would often include a piece of cake or pie. He could just see Bessie standing in the kitchen, humming or singing or talking to herself, and making lunches. Carol liked peanut-butter-and-jelly sandwiches, which he hated. Once, she had taken his lunch by mistake, and when he had opened his bag he was furious. He had expected a bacon-lettuce-and-tomato, which Bessie had promised him.

Gradually, a painful feeling came over him, bringing with it recent memories that became progressively more graphic and clear. He tried to make them go away. He didn't want to think about all that just then. He wasn't in the mood. Closing his eyes, he tried to think about something else. But the feeling was too strong, and it overwhelmed him. He opened his eyes and stared at the ceiling.

IT WAS SIX weeks before. John was still in bed, having fallen back to sleep after the first awakening. He woke in terror. He was late. Jumping up, he got out of his pajamas, put on his underwear, his red-and-blue high socks, corduroy knickers, blue shirt, blue sweater, and brown oxford shoes, and ran into the bathroom, where he quickly washed his face and brushed his teeth. Then he was running downstairs, grabbing his coat and blue stocking cap from a hook in the hall closet, then out the door and into the cold. Too late for breakfast. Too late for goodbyes. Oh, Bessie, you didn't wake me the second time, you lost track of the clock, he thought. Running up the street on a gray, cloudy day, the cold air sharp in his lungs, carrying his books, running for his life. He couldn't be late. Running up hills and down hills. Hilly streets and old houses and trees. He liked to dawdle to school, to take his sweet time. He was late already. Oh, God, he thought, don't let Miss Dornholder give me an hour after school. He ran up a hill, dropped a book, ran back and picked it up, then ran on.

Approaching the old red brick building, the Francis Scott Key School, seeing the empty playground—he was ten minutes late—he suddenly realized that he had forgotten his lunch. Oh no, he thought. He ran into the playground and up the steps, and then, standing breathless in front of the boys' entrance, he wondered if Bessie would bring it up to school. Oh, please don't come, Bessie, he thought. You know what I told you. He hated her to come up with his lunch, as though he was some little boy who couldn't keep things straight. Once, on a rainy day, she had brought his lunch and a pair of rubbers. "Oh, dear God, please don't let her come," he said out loud as he walked into school.

Sitting in class that morning, in the back of the room

near a hanging chart of the navigations of Magellan and Vasco da Gama, he was enraged by the punishment that Miss Dornholder had meted out to him—two hours of penalty time. After school, for two straight days. There was so much that he wanted to do, and after school was the best time. He really hated her.

And he waited for Bessie. He waited for her through the Lord's Prayer, the reading of the Twenty-third Psalm by Emily Ann Green, the pledge of allegiance to the flag, and, before mathematics, the singing of songs—"Old Dog Tray," "Columbia, the Gem of the Ocean," "Old Black Joe," "Dixie," "Carry Me Back to Old Virginny," "Row, Row, Row Your Boat," "Camptown Races," and "My Old Kentucky Home."

You better not come, Bessie, he thought. He would rather starve to death. He looked toward Ewing and Hal, who were up front at opposite ends of a row, wishing he could talk to them. The week before, they had all been together in the back, but Miss Dornholder had split them up.

Time passed. If Bessie was coming, she would be here by now, John thought. With a sense of relief, he felt that he had been saved—that the whole class wouldn't watch silly old Bessie give him his lunch. It would have made Allie Conroy and Freddy Rhodes really happy to see that, he thought, but she wasn't coming, and they could go to h-e-double l. Oh, thank you, God, he thought, moving his lips ever so slightly.

He took a deep breath, smiled, and tried hard to concentrate on mathematics. While he was following a problem in fractions, during a pause between question and answer, he heard a slight tapping on the door pane. He experienced a slight palpitation of the heart. Bessie's face appeared through the glass pane of the upper door. He thought he would die. He tried to convey to her with his most savage, desperate, and angry expression—formed mainly with his mouth and brow—that she had better turn around and keep walking and not bother him. Timidly, with a shy smile, she entered the room. There were titters from a few girls up front. John broke his pencil in half. A shriek, then a strange, high-pitched whine came from the far side of the room. It was Conroy or Rhodes, John thought, feeling weak. Bessie stood near the door, remaining very still, with her head bowed, her shoulders slightly hunched forward, holding the lunch bag in her large brown hands, waiting to be recognized by Miss Dornholder, who, visibly upset by her intrusion, as she had been upset before, ignored her for the moment. John could barely look at her. She wore the red bandanna around her head and an old brown coat that his mother had given her five years before. Standing there, she seemed to be swaying slightly. There was another shriek, followed by general laughter.

"Quiet!" Miss Dornholder said, and then, looking pained and imposed upon, told John to go and get his lunch. "And please be quick about it," she said.

He walked up to the front of the class, trying so hard to be nonchalant that he half tripped. He took his lunch from Bessie and stepped out into the hall with her.

"Oh, damn you, Bessie. I really hate you. I *told* you not to come," he said.

"Johnny, honey, your mama told me to come," she said.

"I don't care," he said. "You promised to eat it on the way if she sent you."

"But, honey, you got to eat."

"Oh, I don't care. You never do what I tell you. Why don't you go away?"

Looking hurt, Bessie turned and walked slowly down the corridor to the stairs. John went into the cloakroom by the hall entrance to put his lunch away on the shelf above his coat. He felt a little ashamed of himself. After he had put his lunch away, he stood with his arms folded. Taking a deep breath, he tried to feel better, but he only felt more sad. While he was standing there, Freddy Rhodes came into the cloakroom. Not seeing John at first, he went directly to the supply closet and pulled out a box of chalk.

John looked at him, feeling sick with hatred. Rhodes' long, straight hair hung down over his forehead. He was large for his age—several inches taller than John and thickly built—with a sullen mouth that was always slightly open. His eyes were dazed and angry. He wore a sweatshirt with "Fort Myer, Va." printed on the front, and a pair of long pants of almost the same shade of corduroy as John's. He had the reputation of being the meanest, toughest boy in the fifth grade. He was about to return to the classroom when he saw John. They stared at one another. Rhodes put the chalk in his pocket, then walked toward John, who unfolded his arms and dropped his hands, slightly cupped, to his sides.

"Just take off, Rhodes," John said.

"Why don't you shut your stupid mouth?"

"I'll shut yours," John said.

Rhodes smiled malevolently. "You sure have a funny old nigger maid," he said.

John's eyes misted over. "You better not say anything about her," he said.

"I'll say what I like about that fat old nigger."

John took a deep breath. "You know what you are, Rhodes? You're a son of a bitch," he said, knowing that that was the worst thing you could call somebody.

Rhodes sucked in some breath and compressed his lips, exposing some upper teeth. "Did you call my mother a dog?" he said, squinting.

"You heard me. She's a mangy old dog like you," John said. "And your sister's an old slut."

Freddy Rhodes hit John hard in the mouth, knocking him down, and John quickly scrambled to his feet, and, swinging wildly, hit Rhodes in the throat. He fell backward, clutching his throat, and John threw himself on him. They rolled over, and Rhodes hit him in the eye, and just as John had his fist back ready to hit Rhodes in the face, Miss Dornholder pulled him to his feet by his ear. He tried to break away from her, but she held him tightly by the collar of his shirt.

"Now, *what happened?*" she said to John.

He didn't say anything.

"Freddy!" she said.

Rhodes wiped his hands on the front of his sweatshirt. "He called me a son of a bitch, and I hit him," he said.

Looking horrified, Miss Dornholder put a hand over her mouth, still holding John by the collar of his shirt with the other. "How awful! Is that true, John?" she said, looking down at him.

"Yes, Ma'am, but—"

"How could you say such a thing?"

"But he—"

"How dare you do such a thing, John—after all your promises?"

"But he insulted Bessie," John said.

She shook her head, then suddenly became livid. "Now, see here. You tell her not ever—not ever again to come into my classroom. Do you understand? She'll stay out in the hall where she belongs and *not* upset my class." She shook him. "And *you!* You will not upset my class. Look at me when I talk to you. I'm so sick—so sick and tired of your foul language."

"I'll get you, Rhodes," John said.

"You're not getting *anyone*. You are going right down to Mr. Pearson's office," Miss Dornholder said. She looked at Freddy Rhodes, who stood there, feeling his throat, with a vague, apprehensive smile on his face. "I'll deal with you later, Freddy. Get inside the room."

He returned to the room. Then Miss Dornholder released her hold on John's collar. "You wait here," she said.

John waited in the cloakroom for Miss Dornholder to write out a note to Mr. Pearson, who was the principal of the school. It was standard procedure. He kept feeling the eye Rhodes had hit; it was a little puffy. He slowly moved his tongue along his lower lip. A barely noticeable clot of blood had formed at the corner of his mouth. He felt fine. It felt wonderful, he thought, to hit someone you hated right in the throat. He thought Rhodes would never forget that punch, and would feel it for days. There was more where that came from.

Miss Dornholder returned with the note in a sealed envelope.

"Now, get going," she said. "And don't you dawdle. I wrote the time down on the note."

The principal's secretary, Miss Cavendish, a tall,

gaunt woman in her forties, immediately took him into Mr. Pearson's office and went out, closing the door. John sat down on a chair in front of Mr. Pearson's desk. A dry, immaculate little man, wearing a blue suit and rimless glasses, Mr. Pearson was going through some papers. He looked up at John briefly, then continued reading. John hated him. He didn't like Miss Cavendish, either. He hadn't ever liked any secretary or teacher in the school except for Wilma Freedy, who had got married and moved to Baltimore. She had taught him in the fourth grade.

After a few minutes, Mr. Pearson looked up from his papers. John tried to look him right in the eye, but he began to feel very light-headed, so he concentrated on Mr. Pearson's blue necktie.

Mr. Pearson appraised John with a look of faint disdain and deep nervous exhaustion. "Give me the note," he said.

John gave him the note. Mr. Pearson took a small silver penknife from his vest pocket and neatly opened the envelope. He read the note, then leaned forward on his desk and folded his small hands. "Now, John, do you know what this means?" he asked.

John didn't say anything.

"You remember what I told you last time," he said.

John looked down at the desk top.

"You've been in here seven times during this term. Five is the limit, but the last time you were sent down I decided to give you one more chance. Now you're in again"—he looked at the note—"for foul language and fighting."

"Sir," John said.

"Please be quiet," Mr. Pearson said, folding his hands over his vest. Leaning back in his chair, he looked up at the ceiling, then picked up a small metal paperweight, stared at it, then put it down. "I'm afraid you've run out of opportunities. I can't give you any more. You're now on probation for a month." He looked somewhat sadly at John. "Now, you know what that means. One more serious mistake and you're expelled."

"But, sir, you didn't even ask me what happened," John said.

"Miss Dornholder told me quite clearly in the note," Mr. Pearson said, looking annoyed.

"This boy insulted our maid," John said, talking rapidly. "And I insulted him back, and then we had a fight. It wasn't all his fault, and it wasn't all *mine*."

Mr. Pearson shook his head and closed his eyes, then, leaning forward, said, "I'm writing to your father today—" John was about to interrupt, but Mr. Pearson raised his hand and went on, "It's not pleasant for me, but I have no choice, you see. Now, let's have no more talk about it. Just make sure you stay out of trouble."

"But, sir," John said.

Mr. Pearson ignored him, and quickly wrote a note to Miss Dornholder telling her that John was on probation. "Take this to your teacher," he said, sliding the note across the desk.

John stayed where he was.

"Now, John, will you please get out of here?" Mr. Pearson said.

Out in the empty school hall, John was so angry he threw the note up in the air and yelled "Damn!" But when the note floated to the floor, he picked it up and put it in his pocket. He began to walk up the stairs, back to his classroom, then stopped and took a deep breath. He felt sick.

WHEN JOHN came out that day, after serving his penalty time, the playground was empty but for Ewing and Hal. They'd been waiting over an hour, leaning against a chain fence. Their books were on the ground. Tall and thin, Ewing wore a leather aviator's cap with one of the flaps turned upward and a heavy black sweater over a blue one. The hood of his red parka turned up over his head, Hal stood with his hands in his front pouch pocket. He was of medium build. He had freckles, and his face was pink. Ewing was pale, with clear blue eyes. Like John, both boys wore knickers and colored socks.

They started the walk home. The day was still cloudy and cold. The route they followed was hilly, with sharp climbs and descents. It was quiet except for the barking of dogs. The trees were bare, and the thin branches on top were bent in the wind. They gave off a sighing, crackling sound. Briefly, the sun broke through the clouds, disappeared, then returned as the clouds began to break. Old wooden houses—white, green, red, and brown—became bright in the sunlight. The boys moved in single file, not talking because of the wind and cold. Soon they broke into a slow trot. After a while, they stopped to rest beside a white board fence. Beyond the fence was a field of tall, wild grass and a few dogwood trees, and then a stretch of lawn that formed an apronlike expanse in front of a large old wooden house.

They decided to climb the fence and take a shortcut home. They raced through the tall grass and across the lawn, past the house, to a small wire fence that separated the property from a little alley where there were garbage cans and a row of private garages. They climbed the fence to the alley and saw a ladder leaning against a garage. Without saying a word, Ewing threw his books on the roof of the garage and went up the ladder. John and Hal followed.

For a while, they ran around the roof, yelling and whooping, and then they picked up small stones from the roof surface and began to throw them at the garbage cans below. While they were in the middle of an accuracy contest—the winner to be the first thrower, using three stones in succession, to hit a garbage can twice and get the other stone into its open top—a heavy-set man wearing a sports coat came running from the old wooden house. "Get the hell off there!" he said.

"We're not bothering anyone," John said, throwing a stone, which missed the can and struck a garage door across the alley.

"You are god-damned well bothering *me*. Now, get down from there or I'm coming up after you," the man said.

John grabbed the top rung of the ladder and tried to pull it up onto the roof, but the man quickly yanked it down.

"I'll break your neck! Now, get off there!" he said.

Holding their books against their chests, the boys climbed down from the roof. John was last. As he stepped down to the alley, the man grabbed him by the shoulders and began to shake him. "You smart little bastard!" he said.

"You let me go," John said. He shook himself free,

dropping a book. He ran off a few steps, then picked up a rock and threw it at the side window of the garage There was a crash of shattered glass. The boys continued running for a quarter of a mile before daring to look back.

On the following morning, the owner of the garage telephoned Mr. Pearson, informing him that a boy who had dropped a library book belonging to the school—*The Pathfinder,* by James Fenimore Cooper, checked out on February 4th—had thrown a rock through his garage window. He demanded restitution.

John's identity was immediately traced. Pale and forlorn, he was called into Mr. Pearson's office.

After a brief interrogation, Mr. Pearson looked at him coldly. "John, you are no longer a student at this school," he said. "You will turn in your books at once, and then go right home."

Feeling sick, John left without a word, passing Miss Cavendish, who regarded him with stony silence.

For a brief time, he stood in the empty hallway outside the principal's office, feeling light and dizzy, and then he returned to his classroom. Without saying a word to anyone, without a glance at Ewing or Hal, he cleared the books out of his desk, then went into the cloakroom and picked up his coat, hat, and lunch. He went down to the library, in the basement, turned in his books, received a receipt, and left the school.

He didn't go home. He spent part of the day in the woods. Carrying his lunch, he walked for miles through the deep woods, following the foot and bridle paths, which he knew well, and then striking out along the creek. The day was sunny and cold, but he could see rain clouds far off. At times, he would follow the creek, walking beside it through fallen leaves, or he would stand on a rock in the middle of the rushing water and try to see how far down the creek he could move, hopping from rock to rock. Once, he slipped, his leg going into the water up to the knee. He turned up the wet elastic of his knicker and removed his sock and shoe. He put the wet sock in the pocket of his coat, and then he dried his leg with leaves. He poured the water out of his shoe and then put it back on. It was very uncomfortable.

At about one o'clock, he became hungry, and he sat down on a fallen tree in a small, sunny clearing and opened his brown bag. Bessie had put in some fried chicken and a piece of cake and a half-pint bottle of milk. He ate slowly.

After finishing his lunch, he wiped his mouth with his handkerchief, then put the chicken bones, wax paper, and milk bottle into the bag. He took a pencil out of his pocket and wrote on the bag, "John Lionel, Feb. 6, 1940. Thrown out of school." He put the bag between two fallen logs and covered it with a flat stone to protect it from the rain. Someday, I'll come back and find it, he thought. He was surprised how good he felt. It was wonderful to have the whole day to do exactly as he pleased. He laughed out loud, then suddenly stood up and threw a handful of leaves up in the air and stood under them as they came down. He found some perfect throwing stones and, climbing part way up a hill, threw them into the creek.

A little later, as he walked along a dirt path, his foot quite wet and cold, he became despondent. They would all be waiting for him at home, he thought. He wished he didn't have to go home, but there was nowhere else to go. He suddenly wished he could be on a horse out West on the prairie somewhere, riding to a friendly place. Bessie and Ewing and Hal would be waiting for him, along with some wonderful Indian friends they had made. They'd sit around a campfire and sing and tell stories. He continued to think in this way. It made him very happy until he realized he wasn't on any horse and, no matter what, he'd have to go home eventually and face the music. Becoming more despondent than ever, he tried not to think of his father.

At about a quarter after two in the afternoon, John came out of the woods and took a bus to the Smithsonian Institution, spending the rest of the day in the Indian Exhibit. He enjoyed it very much.

IT WAS DARK when John arrived home. Tired and frightened, he entered the house through the kitchen door. Bessie was preparing a platter of vegetables when she saw him.

"Honey, where you *been?* They all eating."

John looked down at the floor.

"Where's your sock?" she said, looking at his leg, still covered with bits of leaves.

He pulled the sock out of his pocket and handed it to her. Looking concerned, she smiled at him. "Don't you worry none. I know whatever happen it ain't your fault," she said, giving him a quick hug. "Your daddy been home since two o'clock looking for you. The school telephoned him. He been *stalking* around. You know his temper. He say they thrown you out. He saying *plenty*. . . ." She patted John's face. "I going to give you a little food. Now, you go on up to your room, tippy-toe like, and I tell him that you home but ain't hungry. After you finishes eating, put the plate under the bed. Maybe he calm down some. Now, don't forget to clean yourself up. You know how he get about that."

She quickly put a roll, a slice of warm pot roast, and some potatoes on a plate and handed it to him. John went quietly out the door to the hall and upstairs to his room.

While he ate, he heard his father yelling in the dining room below. Bessie must have told him I'm home, John thought. He hurriedly ate the roll and a little more pot roast, then put the half-empty plate under his bed, and ran to the bathroom and cleaned up. Then he returned to his room and sat on the edge of his bed and waited.

When his father came into the room, John couldn't look at him. His father grabbed him under his arms and pulled him to his feet.

"Where in the hell have you been?" he said.

John didn't say anything.

"I'm talking to you! Where were you?"

"In the woods," John said, barely audible.

"What do you mean, 'in the woods'?"

John looked at his father, then at the floor. His father's face was stricken with anger and disappointment.

"There's something wrong with you," his father said.

John nodded.

"Well?"

John didn't say anything.

"You're out!" his father said.

John took a deep breath and looked at the globe on his desk.

"How does it feel to get kicked out!"

John was afraid he was going to be beaten. If his father hit him, he would never speak to him again. If that's the way he wants it, then he can hit me, John thought.

"Well, what do you have to say for yourself?" his father asked.

John took a deep breath. "Daddy, this boy called Bessie an old nigger, and then I called him something, and then—"

"Shut up! You broke this man's window. *That's* why they threw you out."

"But I was telling you about *probation.*"

"I'm not interested in your excuses. I know how you cursed that boy," he said.

"But, Daddy—"

"Shut up. You just want to break windows and curse and act like a rowdy, is that it?"

"No!" John yelled.

His father slapped him and said, "You make me sick!"

John didn't say anything.

"Do you hear me? Answer me!"

"Oh, Daddy, I don't care!" John said.

His father slapped him hard in the face.

It stung worse than the first time. Fighting back the tears, he tried to pretend that his father wasn't even there. He was never going to speak to him again. He would die first. His face was burning, and it was hard to breathe. He was going to be very nonchalant. It was a word that he had learned from Ewing, and he kept thinking, nonchalant, nonchalant. At the same time, he wondered if he was going to get whipped with the belt.

"I'm sick of you," his father said. "We're all sick of you." And then he left the room.

John sat down on the bed, and put his face in

his hands. Then he sat up straight and, making a fist, whirled and hit the bed as hard as he could. He removed a shoe and threw it against the wall. Then he slowly undressed, trying very hard to be nonchalant. He put on his pajamas and got into bed and turned off the lamp on his night table. He lay there in the dark, his face stinging with rage and sorrow. "Oh, damn it to hell. I don't care," he said. He broke momentarily into sobs, then stifled them. "I don't give a good damn," he said. He sat up quickly and hit the pillow, and then fell back down. Gradually, he dropped off to sleep.

About three in the morning, feeling warm and feverish, John woke up. It was raining. He could hear the rain on the windows. He got out of bed and looked out. The faint light from the street lamps lay softly on the trees. Puddles on the sidewalk were splashing from the rain. Here and there mist rose from the lawns. He sat down on a chair by the window. He didn't feel well. The room felt close and uncomfortable. Very warm and slightly numb, he got up from the chair and walked somewhat unsteadily out of the room. The house was dark. Holding on to the banister, he moved slowly down the stairs and turned on a small lamp in the hall. It was quiet but for the ticking of the grandfather's clock. He went into the kitchen, opened the back door, and then, wearing only his pajamas, stepped out into the back yard as though it were the most natural thing in the world. He walked slowly, feeling shock at the cold wetness on his bare feet. It was a cold, hard rain, and he was quickly soaked. He stood on the grass and closed his eyes. After a few minutes, he sat down, looking at the darkened houses. He began to shiver. His pajamas clung to his body.

After about fifteen minutes, feeling frightened, his

teeth chattering, he decided to go inside. He went up the stairs, got out of his wet pajamas, took a towel from the linen closet, and frantically wiped himself dry. Then he put on his knickers and bathrobe and got back into bed. His lips were purple. He fell into a stuporous sleep and awoke a few hours later, coughing and shaking violently.

The doctor came in the morning. John had pneumonia. In the days that followed, he nearly died. When news of his illness reached his school, he was, as an incentive to his recovery—as an act of mercy—reinstated in good standing.

THE SUNLIGHT was streaming into the room. Bessie came in with his lunch—hot pea soup, a grilled-cheese sandwich, and a glass of orange juice. While she straightened out his bed, he sat on a chair and ate from the tray she had put on the small table. "You started your back work, honey?" Bessie asked.

"Oh, Bessie, you're so nice and brown!" John said, suddenly smiling.

"Now, that ain't nice."

"How's Hamp?" John asked.

"Aw, Hampton he ain't nothing. Don't talk to me about him," she said. "You done your back work? Your mama wants to know."

"I can't do it all in one morning," John said.

"You started?"

"No," John said, reaching out and grabbing her by the arm. "Thanks for the grilled cheese, Bessie."

She leaned against the closet door and put a hand over her eyes.

"Are you tired?" John asked.

"I guess so."

"Why don't you sit down?"

"If I sit down, I afraid I can't get up," she said. She took a deep breath, then sighed. "Honey, your mama working me to death."

John put down his sandwich and looked annoyed. "Bessie, tell her you're no slave."

Bessie laughed. "You want to get me killed?"

"Now, listen—"

He suddenly stopped talking. His mother, wearing a heavy tweed coat, walked briskly into the room.

She looked equivocally at John. "I'm going out for a while. Do you want anything?"

John shook his head.

"Do we need anything in the house, Bessie?" she asked.

"No, Ma'am," Bessie said.

"You always say no, and we always run out of things," John's mother said. "You're the most *disorganized* person."

"Yes, Ma'am," Bessie said.

John took a sip of orange juice and stared at the tabletop. His mother stood in the center of the room, setting one foot forward and slightly raising the toe of her high-heeled shoe. During a silence that lasted for almost half a minute, she appeared vaguely distraught, with a wary and persecuted look that, in their combined presence, had become natural to her. She said to Bessie, "I know you've been talking about me."

"Why, Miss Mary!" Bessie said.

"Oh, you be quiet. I knew you'd deny it."

Bessie began to edge slowly toward the door. His

mother looked at her. "Where do you think you're going?"

"I got my work to do," Bessie said.

"Oh, now you're so anxious about your *work*. Now you just stay put." She looked at John and patted a stray wisp of hair into place. "I heard you *both* talking. I was standing outside the door." She looked at Bessie. "So I work you to death."

"Oh, you listened," John said.

"I *overheard,*" his mother said. She unbuttoned her coat and began to take it off. "Oh, will you help me, Bessie?" Bessie helped her off with her coat. "We're going to have it out right now."

She nervously touched her forehead, then clasped her hands in front of her. "Now, Bessie," she said, nodding in John's direction. "I want you to tell Abraham Lincoln over there something."

Bessie smiled, then looked down at the coat she was holding.

"Now, are you a slave?"

"No, Ma'am."

"Oh, yes, you are," John said.

"I'm talking to Bessie," his mother said. "Now, please be quiet." She glared at him. "Now Bessie, who takes care of your doctor bills and lends you money—and never gets paid back?"

"Now, I going to pay you back," Bessie said, looking hurt.

"Oh, be quiet. I'm not asking for the money," his mother said. "Now, can you *possibly* remember who sends you a turkey every Thanksgiving *and* Christmas?"

"You do, Miss Mary."

"Well, *thank* you," his mother said. She looked briefly at John, and then asked, "Now, Bessie, do you get low wages?"

Bessie looked down and smiled weakly.

"I'm talking to you, Bessie!"

"They ain't low," Bessie said. "But they ain't high, either."

His mother, looking pained, unclasped her hands, then clasped them again. "Now, you listen to me. I bet there's not a maid in Washington who gets more. I was talking to Ewing's mother"—she glanced at John—"about their Martha. She's a friend of yours, Bessie, so you can ask her. Well, you get more than *she* gets, and do you know how long Martha's been in that family? *Forty* years. She came up with them from North Carolina, and she's just the *sweetest* person. She never complains, and she never acts surly or sulky like someone else I know—like this very *second,* Bessie. You should see the expression on your face."

Bessie sighed, briefly put a hand over her mouth, then looked down at the floor.

"She looks all right," John said, getting up from his chair. He sat down on the edge of the bed.

"You would take up for her. Naturally," his mother said. She smoothed her dress, then took a small handkerchief from its sleeve. "You take up for her and she takes up for you. It's wonderful." She dabbed her eyes. "So I'm not good to you, Bessie. Is that it?"

"Miss Mary, you're very good to me," Bessie said.

"Oh, say the truth!" John said.

"Now, John, honey," Bessie said. "Your mama's very good to me."

His mother touched her eyes lightly with her handkerchief, then looked at Bessie. "You used to show me such affection—such kindness and affection—"

"Now, Miss Mary, you know I love you," Bessie said, walking over and putting an arm around her and pulling her head gently to her shoulder. "You my sweet madam. You know I love you. I love this whole *family*."

His mother held Bessie's arm, then disengaged herself, wiping her eyes. "Well, just be nicer," she said. Then she looked somewhat wistfully at John. "You could *both* show me a little more kindness," she said.

"But, Bessie," John said, shaking his head, "how about your vacation? You know you want two weeks. How about your raise?"

Bessie half smiled, then looked at the floor.

His mother asked for her coat. Bessie held it for her. Buttoning her coat, she came over to John, who, feeling strangely unsettled by his mother's beauty and emotion and her talent for confusing what had seemed so clear, let himself be kissed.

When she left, John yawned and got into bed. He closed his eyes. In a few minutes, he was fast asleep. Bessie, who had left with his mother, came into his room and, finding him asleep, pulled down the blinds and drew the curtains.

She woke him two hours later. He felt wonderful—light and happy. She drew a bath for him. After he bathed, he got into fresh pajamas. Bessie made him put on his bathrobe, with a towel tucked in around his neck. She brought him a cup of tea with lemon.

While he was reading *Treasure Island*, Ewing and Hal arrived. He heard them yelling in the street. There was a loud rapping at the front door; then he heard Bessie open it and say, "Well, if it ain't the James Boys."

They ran upstairs and into his room. John smiled widely but with a trace of shyness. It was a little strange to see them. They looked so different, John thought, and they seemed to have grown, particularly Ewing. John was so glad to see them that he could hardly talk.

He and Hal shook hands, and Ewing slapped him on the back.

"You look white as a sheet," Ewing said, unzipping his jacket.

"I'm all better," John said.

Hal pulled his red parka off over his head, and sat down on a chair by the bed. Ewing tore off his leather aviator's cap and threw it on the desk. They all smiled back and forth, without saying much. Then, as Ewing took off his jacket, he said, "Say, Johnny, what animal has eyes and can't see and legs and can't walk, but can jump as high as the Washington Monument?"

John thought, and then said, "I don't know, Ewing. What?"

"A wooden horse," Ewing said, looking at Hal.

"But a wooden horse can't jump," John said.

"It can jump as high as the Washington Monument, which can't jump, either," Ewing said.

"Oh lord, Ewing, that's neat!" John said, smiling.

"Say," Ewing said. "Did you hear this joke? There was this elevator boy, and this lady said to him, 'Don't you get tired, son?' and this boy said, 'Yes, ma'am,' and she said, 'What makes you so tired? Is it going up?' and he said, 'No, ma'am,' and she said, 'Then is it going down?' and he said, 'No, ma'am.' 'Then what is it that makes you so tired?' she says, and this boy says, 'All the questions, ma'am.' "

John laughed so hard that he began to cough. Hal slapped him on the back, and Ewing called Bessie, who had to bring John a glass of water. John then told Bessie the joke, and she said, smiling, "Honey, that's pretty good." Then she went back to work.

"Bessie's really neat," Ewing said.

Hal said everyone missed him at school, even Miss Dornholder.

"And Mr. Pearson misses you," Ewing said, smiling. "He misses seeing you in his office. I was sent there yesterday, and he *told* me."

John and Hal laughed.

"We met your mother, near the grocery store," Hal said.

"She's really pretty," Ewing said.

John nodded, then picked up his baseball glove and pounded the pocket.

"It won't be long now," he said.

"You said it," Ewing said. "We played catch on that warm day last week. Hal can throw a curve."

"I just learned all of a sudden," Hal said.

"Oh, that's great!" John said.

Ewing said that he had spoken to Ollie Parker, the coach of the Federal Vacuum Cleaner Peewee Team. "He's going to play you at third or short, Johnny, and me at second, and Hal's going to catch, and the Elbertson brothers are playing the outfield. We'll have a great team."

"They're measuring for uniforms in about two weeks," Hal said.

John felt extremely happy. Ollie had once told him that he had a lot of potential.

"I bet Washington makes the first division," Ewing said, putting on John's glove.

"Bucky Harris says he needs more pitching," Hal said.

"Well, we've got Travis," John said. "He'll just knock in more runs."

"He's great," Ewing said. "And so is Buddy Lewis."

"We always fold against the Yankees," Hal said.

"Not always," John said.

They played checkers—a round-robin tournament. Hal won. Ewing came in third. John was desolated when, playing for the championship of Northwest Washington, Hal forced him to jump, setting up a four-way jump by Hal's king. Seeing John was crushed, Hal said he'd take it over, but John shook his head. "Boy, was I *stupid!*" he said, looking morose. Ewing and Hal began to laugh, and then John began to laugh, too, and before long, without any further reason for merriment, they were hysterical.

Bessie heard a lot of laughing and screaming from the room. She served them milk and chocolate cake, and Ewing and Hal left about five-thirty.

AFTER DINNER, Bessie stopped in John's room to say good night. "See you in the morning, honey. You take it slow and easy," she said, bending over his bed. He hugged her and then lay back.

"You better not be late," he said.

Bessie left. She was going home to her own children. He felt he loved her more than anyone he'd ever known. She was the kindest, most wonderful person in the world, and he was her "white child." Lying there, he couldn't ever remember being so happy in his whole life. He had no desire to use foul language. His mind was filled with pleasant impressions. He was getting better. He'd be out there soon with Ewing and Hal, playing third or short for Federal Vacuum Cleaner. He'd move like a big cat. He looked forward to the spring and summer afternoons. Feelings of love overwhelmed him.

Closing his eyes, he imagined meeting Freddy Rhodes in the street, and he said, "Hi, Rhodes, how are you doing?" His manner was friendly and nonchalant, not at all "extreme," and Rhodes was terribly surprised by his friendliness and became a new person.

John basked in a glow of redemption. Then it all seemed false. He knew he would fight Rhodes again. In his mind, the school playground came into view. He was on it, and he was fighting Freddy Rhodes. Freddy threw a hard punch, but John neatly ducked and threw a perfectly timed right to the jaw, and Rhodes went down to the ground.

An incredible gladness swept over John. "You had it coming, Freddy," he said, "but I don't hate you."

He felt wonderful all evening, and when his father stopped in for a little talk, John smiled with delight.

A NOTE ABOUT THE AUTHOR

JULIAN MAZOR was born in Baltimore, Maryland, in 1929, and raised there and in Washington, D.C. He is a graduate of Indiana University and Yale Law School. *Washington and Baltimore* is his first published book. His stories have appeared in *Shenandoah* and *The New Yorker*.

A NOTE ON THE TYPE

THE TEXT of this book is set in Caledonia, a typeface designed by W(illiam) A(ddison) Dwiggins for the Mergenthaler Linotype Company in 1939. Dwiggins chose to call his new typeface Caledonia, the Roman name for Scotland, because it was inspired by the Scotch types cast about 1833 by Alexander Wilson & Son, Glasgow type founders. However, there is a calligraphic quality about this face that is totally lacking in the Wilson types. Dwiggins referred to an even earlier typeface for this "liveliness of action"—one cut around 1790 by William Martin for the printer William Bulmer. Caledonia has more weight than the Martin letters, and the bottom finishing strokes (serifs) of the letters are cut straight across, without brackets, to make sharp angles with the upright stems, thus giving a "modern face" appearance.

Composed, printed, and bound by
The Colonial Press Inc., Clinton, Massachusetts

Typography and binding design by
Kenneth Miyamoto